PERFECT TRAGEDY

MASON CREEK #5

JENNIFER MILLER

To my Papa Rush. Because the very presence of you made everyone feel extraordinarily complete and more loved than you can possibly imagine. We miss you every single day.

$\mathcal{T}$here are moments in life that define time and space. Moments so significant that suddenly everything else becomes about before it and after it. It's crazy that when they're happening, we're clueless about how momentous the situations will be. Honestly, I'm still not sure which hit harder, my head when it smacked against the ground upon falling from the large sycamore tree in my front yard or the reaction to meeting the dark-haired, green-eyed boy that caused my fall. After that day everything became about before I met Blake and after - the moment truly defining my life, forever.

Thinking back on that day will always make me smile. The excitement, the innocence, the energy. What I wouldn't give to have the same energy I had as a nine-year-old child. I can still see myself running through my yard, grass in need of a mowing tickling my ankles while I'm completely focused on my destination. Sun warms my face and there's a breeze in the air making the wisps of hair that have fallen out of my ponytail stroke my cheeks. I can't help the laugh that bubbles up from within me, the excitement unable to be contained. My brother's binoculars, taken from his room without permission, bounce against my chest like a drum of doom pounding out the trouble I'm sure to be in when he finds out. But taking them was necessary, important even, I remind myself in a self-justifying way.

When I reach the large sycamore tree at the edge of our property, I begin climbing up the wood planks that are nailed to the trunk creating a makeshift ladder, enthusiastically. The bark scrapes my knees and leaves traces under my fingernails as I climb pulling myself higher until I reach the bottom of the treehouse my dad built. Pushing up the bottom, I pull myself up and inside, quickly closing the hatch. Moving the few steps to the window, I look through the leaves partially obscuring my vision and quickly put the binoculars up to my eyes and peer over at our neighbor's house, squinting when the sun momentarily blinds me and makes me see spots.

Squeezing my eyelids open and closed a few times, I shake my head attempting to make the spots disappear before peering through the binoculars yet again. My eyes move over the tops of the wheat field, the ripening heads of wheat swaying in the wind like they're dancing to music only they can hear. When my eyes finally find what they've been searching for, I view the house next door. A little squeak leaves me when I see what I've been waiting for - a moving truck.

When old Mr. Leonard, the previous owner, kicked the bucket, it was all anyone in our small town talked about for days. You would have thought his passing was a scandal for all the attention it caused, rather than just an old man that had no one in his life. Because of that, it took them several days to find him after he died. It didn't take long before the next topic up for discussion was who would purchase his home when it went up for sale. A pretty yellow house with white shutters on an acre property, it was sure to be a treasure for some lucky family. My favorite thing about the house was the bright red front door that perfectly matched the big barn situated in the back. I also happened to know from personal experience that one of the best tree swings could be found in their back yard. I begged my dad to hang one from our tree, but he said the poor tree already had a house in it; what more did we want.

With a sigh I lower the binoculars from my eyes when I don't detect any movement around the property and turn to grab one of the folding chairs. Placing it in front of the window I take a seat, my eyes peeled on the house, and think about the day my mom came back from the hair salon, Serenity, after having had a stylish hair cut, with the big news. Mom told dad that her hairstylist, Anna, heard from a client of hers, who heard from the friend of the town's real estate agent Grady's cousin, that the house had finally sold. Our attention spiked; Jack and I consumed every word of their conversation. Each day after, we'd hoped to find out the answer to the big question: will there be any kids our age that will finally live next door?

The suspense may very well kill me. My knee bounces up and down and I chew on my nails while placing the binoculars back to my eyes and do another perfunctory sweep of the property. Still nothing. I wonder how long it will take Jack to figure out where I am. Not long I imagine. There's only a few places he'd need to look. I love my brother, he's my best friend, but our relationship is fairly one-sided. All we ever do is play whatever he wants to play and do whatever he wants to do. Video games, tag, nerf guns, building a fort, army men, or throwing around a football are some of his favorites. I take pride in the fact that I can do anything a boy can do, if not better (well some things for sure) but sometimes when I'm alone in my room I like to do what Jack calls 'girly things'. I pretend I'm a princess in a deep sleep waiting for a kiss from her prince. I pretend I'm a ballerina on stage with lights displaying every move I make while an audience watches with bated breath. Other times I'll turn on some music and have a dance party or put on makeup and my mom's high heels and pretend I'm a runway model. One time Jack caught me and teased me for days. My cheeks still flush red when I think about it.

Jack and I have spent days making sure we tuned into our parents' boring conversations for any news about our new neighbors. We've spent hours discussing if there would be kids, if they'd be our ages, practicing how we should introduce ourselves, determining the first game we'd play. And then this morning I finally heard the magic words "moving truck." I immediately ran to Jack's room and tried to wake him, but he just groaned at me and rolled over. Not willing nor patient enough to wait, I wasted no time grabbing his binoculars and coming here on my own. If you snooze you lose. He'll be mad for sure, but being able to brag that I knew something he didn't will be worth it.

It's as if the thought alone brings him to me. "Sienna!"

Jumping in my seat guiltily, I immediately take the binoculars and hide them under a couple of blankets in the corner.

"Sienna!"

"What?" I lean out the window and look down seeing him standing at the bottom of the tree with his hands on his hips.

"I can't believe you didn't wake me!"

"I tried!"

He scoffs.

"I did!" I declare and stomp my foot for emphasis.

"Well you didn't try very hard then."

"Did too," I argue.

He grumbles and I hear him start climbing up the tree to join me. "I knew as soon as I heard mom and dad talking about the new neighbors that I'd find you here."

"Well duh. What do you want, an award?"

I catch the roll of his eyes as he comes through the hatch. He leaves it open and moves to stand next to my chair.

"Well, do you see anyone or what? Tell me what's going on."

"No, I haven't seen anyone. The truck is there though."

"Hm, maybe the moving truck got here first and the family will come later or something, but that's good."

"Why is that good?"

"Because mom said I had to come get you and we need to go do our chores."

"What? Now?" I whine.

"Yep, come on, she wasn't messing around. She had her serious face on."

I sigh, "But we might miss something."

"We'll be fast."

With one last look of longing next door, I carefully climb down the tree and run across the yard with my brother toward our barn. Our house, unlike the one next door is blue. We also have a large barn behind it, but it's just a boring 'ol white one - not at all as fun as red. We run past the large garden our mom and dad have spent hours tending, and then fly past our cherry trees too. Most kids likely hate their chores, but we don't mind ours because our chores mean taking care of the animals we have on our property. Five horses, two goats, six chickens, two dogs, and one barn cat. She's pregnant though and mom says it won't be long and we'll have a litter of kittens. At least for a while. Mom is already reminding us that we will not be able to keep them all.

Aside from harvesting our wheat field, which is no small feat, we sell the fruit from our trees at the local farmer's market and sometimes mom will sell vegetables from our garden too. Even with lots of canning we grow more than we could ever consume alone so we add it to our wares for selling. We even have neighbor friends that will come by our house and pick them up because they don't want to chance them getting sold out at market. Mom and dad give Jack and I money from our sales for our hard work helping and we usually take it and spend it at The Sweet Spot Bakery or the Twisted Sisters Ice Cream Shack.

When it's time for our wheat to be harvested, sometimes my dad will let me sit on his lap while he drives the combine. It's awesome watching the large machine reap, thresh and winnow all the wheat. It's a big job and my favorite is when big trucks come to our property to pick up orders to help ship it out. Dad says it goes all over the United States and we like to spend time guessing and making up stories about where it's headed after it's picked up and all the things that it becomes.

In the summer, we also organize horseback riding trail rides and tours which are a big hit with tourists and locals alike. Some couples like to have what they call romantic date nights which is just gross, but mom says it's the people that come during the summer months for some "country living" that really helps "butter our bread" - whatever that means.

Walking into the barn I head to the bag of chicken feed and scoop some into the tin cup. Walking it to the chicken pen to feed them, I laugh as they come running after hearing the feed hit against the tin cup.

Feeding all the animals takes a little longer that I'd like but I can't help but visit with them a little while I take care of them. Finished, I'm just about to grab Jack so we can run back to the treehouse to continue our spy mission when I hear our mother calling for us.

Stepping out of the barn, I immediately see her walking toward me. Dressed in jeans and a blue t-shirt, she has her long dark hair pulled out of her face into a braid that hangs over her shoulder. Her doctor's bag is clutched in her hand, making it clear she's gotten a call that she needs to answer.

"Sienna," she says my name again.

"What?" I ask impatiently, my mind already on wondering if the new neighbors have finally showed up yet.

"Manners, Sienna."

"Sorry," I mumble apologetically. "I meant to say, yes?"

Her mouth turns up at the corners as if she finds me amusing, "That's better. I'm on my way to the Fox's house. Jinxy, their cow, is about to give birth. Do you want to tag along?"

My nose wrinkles at the thought of watching the Fox's cow give birth. I've seen a horror birth show before when one of our own barn cats, Snow White, had a litter of kittens. It's really not an experience I care to repeat. In fact, I usually think twice about petting her now. Mom, our town's veterinarian, kept calling it the "miracle of life," but all I saw was a seriously gross situation I try to force out of my mind whenever I see her.

"No, thank you, mom. Jack and I are going to see what we can find out about our new neighbors," I admit.

And that was a mistake.

Putting her hands on her hips she gives me a stern warning, "Don't you two go over there being nosey. Moving is hard and busy enough, they don't need a couple of kids getting in the way. I already told you that we'll go over there together at some point, after they get settled a bit, and introduce ourselves, okay?"

"We won't, mom, I promise. We're just going to watch. From the treehouse."

"Fine, but that's as close as you get."

"Promise," I nod.

"Where's your brother?"

"Here!" Jack yells popping his head out of the barn making it clear he was listening to our whole conversation. "Hi, mom."

"Did you hear all that?" She's no fool.

"Yes," he admits.

"Alright then, stay out of trouble you two. Don't be a nuisance to your father, either. He has a lot on his plate today, okay?"

"Okay," we agree in chorus.

"I'll be back in a little while," she calls over her shoulder as she walks away.

Jack and I close up the barn and make sure all the animals are fine and then we dash back to the treehouse as soon as we're finished. Looking up into the branches, I smile, excitement making my stomach flip.

Without a word Jack begins to climb. Once he's up and inside, I follow, leaving the hatch open. I've concocted a plan to vacate quickly once we see their arrival and get first dibs. Jack is clueless. He's already at the window looking across toward our neighbor's house. Immediately, I grab the binoculars from their hiding place in my excitement forgetting that I'm going to have some explaining to do. As soon as Jack sees them he does a double take and emits a mixed sound of surprise and annoyance.

"You took those from my room without asking?"

"I told you that I tried to wake you up."

"That doesn't mean you can just take things when you want." He holds out his hand, "Give them to me."

"Fine," I sigh reluctantly knowing arguing is futile and not wanting him to stay angry. Jack may only be a year older than I am, but he uses every one of those twelve months to his complete advantage. Plus, the boy can ignore me like it's an olympic sport; and if they awarded metals, he'd have earned a gold several times. I hate it with a passion.

Even though I aggravated him, he smiles at me once the binoculars are in his hands. The excitement in his eyes matches my own. I smile in return, and watch avidly as he puts them to his eyes and looks over at the house thinking our weeks of curiosity is about to be answered.

Watching his face closely, eager for any sign of news, I look toward the house on my own and squint. Immediately I see that other cars have arrived and I gasp in excitement. "What do you see?"

"Shh," is his only response.

Frowning, I look back toward the house just in time to see some people walk out of the house and toward the car. I can't make out any specific details, but they head to the car's trunk and lean inside.

"Give them to me now, it's my turn."

"No. In a minute. I'm not done yet."

"Come on, Jack. I want to see too."

"There's really nothing for you to see. There's a girl, but she looks like she's older than me."

Something in his voice makes me instantly more curi-ous. He's got a slight smile on his face and I swear the binoculars are going to make his eyeballs pop out the other end because he has them pressed to them incredibly hard.

Even more curious now, I grab hold of the strap and pull. He's not expecting it and they come flying away from his face and into my hands, "Yes!"

He protests, but I'm too busy devouring the sight before me and it too has captured my interest. A pretty girl with bright pink hair holds a box tight in her hands as she moves from the car's trunk toward the house. Her ample breasts sit on top of the box she's holding, practically falling out of her shirt. I may only be ten, but I know exactly what my eleven year-old brother was looking at. He's in love at first sight. Stupid. I snicker under my breath.

A woman steps out of the house and says something to the girl I had just been watching. She must be her mother. She's talking and pointing at something inside. Before I can look around to see if there's anyone else, Jack yanks on the strap trying to take the binoculars from my hands. I should have expected he'd get impatient and want them back, but he manages to surprise me.

"Stop! I'm not finished yet!"

"Give them back."

"No! Your turn was longer than mine. I'm not done yet."

"They're my binoculars," he pulls them again.

"Don't be stupid, I've had them for less than five minutes!" I yank them hard again, not willing to be bossed around.

"What are you looking at?" An unfamiliar voice asks loudly from below and it completely takes me off guard. It clearly takes Jack by surprise too because he lets go of the strap.

I fall, and I fall just right. Or wrong. Take your pick. I fall perfectly through the open hatch.

Branches scrape against my skin and snag my clothes as I pass by them on my way to the ground.

Sooner than I expect, I land. Hard.

I'm so startled, I simply lay there.

"Shit!" I hear Jack curse and I immediately think how mad my dad would be if he knew. We aren't allowed to curse, but that leaves my mind instantly as I become aware of three things simultaneously.

One, there's a trickle of blood running down the side of my face from above my eye.

Two, my head hurts where it bounced off the ground and there's a sharp pain in my wrist. I think I should be happy I didn't split my head open, but I'm positive I'm going to have one heck of a headache.

Three, there's a boy, that's not Jack, standing over me.

At least, I'm pretty sure he is. Maybe I hit my head harder than I realize. The sun is right at his back and it's difficult to make out any of his features. Maybe I'm wrong and it isn't a boy, it's an angel and I just died falling from this tree.

Panic begins to enter my chest for a brief moment until I hear Jack curse again as he scrambles down the tree. This validates I'm still earth bound because I'm confident there's no cursing allowed in heaven.

"Are you okay?" The boy asks me.

"I-I-I-don't-"

"I'm sorry," he says. "I didn't mean to scare you." He shifts and I can see his face a little more fully now and W-O-W what a face. He must be an angel on earth, because I'm sure I've never seen a boy that looks like that.

"Don't move!" Jack orders as his head joins the other standing over me. "You're bleeding," he states the obvious and looks around helplessly. "I need to get something to wipe the blood away and see how bad it is."

"My wrist hurts," I croak and turn my head to see my brother pick leaves from the tree. Scrunching my nose at him I prepare to tell him that's not going to work, but before I can, the boy who is still standing over me pulls a cloth from his pocket. Bending down, he gently presses it to the cut at my brow.

"Does it hurt very bad?"

"No," I lie not wanting to sound like a sissy.

"Oh, thank you," Jack says to the boy noticing his help. Kneeling down he pulls the cloth away from the cut and frowns. "I think you may need stitches."

"Mom's going to be mad," I tell him.

"Who are you?" Jack asks looking at the boy.

He answers Jack, but doesn't take his eyes from me. "I'm Blake. I'm moving in next door," he points in the direction of his house as if we don't know where he's referring. "We were told that kids my age lived next door and so I walked over to see if you were outside." He pauses and then finally breaks eye contact with me and looks at Jack, "Were you..." he looks at the binoculars now on the ground. "Spying on us?"

I feel my face flush, but Jack simply shrugs unembarrassed, "We were curious about who was moving in. Unlike you, we weren't told if there were any kids, let alone one our age."

"Can I help you up?" Blake asks me.

"She's okay, aren't you Sienna?"

Blake ignores Jack and reaches down to me anyway. When he takes my hand, it hurts my wrist and I hiss in pain. He immediately pulls away and reaches for my other hand instead. "I think you hurt your wrist too," he says.

Biting my lip, I feel very aware of his hand in mine. My

body aches and feels incredibly sore. He holds onto my arms and makes sure I'm steady before letting go. Looking up, I finally get an even better look at Blake.

Dark hair so thick it looks like a helmet, green eyes like the grass he stands on shaded with dark lashes. A dusting of freckles that tells me he enjoys long hours outdoors cover his nose and cheeks.

"Thank you," I finally manage and he smiles at me.

That smile. It lights up his whole face and makes my tummy flip in a way I don't quite understand.

"So, you guys are moving in today, huh?" Jack asks the obvious, completely forgetting about me at the moment. It takes Blake's attention away from me which makes me frown.

"We are."

"I saw a girl too, that your sister?"

"Yes, my older sister, Mandy. It's just the two of us and our parents."

"Same here. Just me, Sienna and our parents. How old are you?"

"Almost twelve."

"Me too," Jack says excitedly. "Hey, do you like to play video games?"

"They're my favorite, I play them all the time. Why? Do you? What's your favorite game?"

I tune them out, the pain from my fall becoming more apparent by the minute. "Jack?" I say but he ignores me, too distracted by his new friend.

"Do you want to go play?" Jack asks with excitement.

"Sure," Blake replies but then his eyes catch mine.

"Awesome, let's go!" Jack says and takes a few steps toward our house.

Blake starts to follow then stops suddenly. "Oh, wait. We

need to get your sister home and looked at. She's hurt."

"Oh, yeah."

"Thanks for remembering," I roll my eyes.

"Do you need help, Sienna, or are you fine?" His tone makes it clear that he wants my answer to be 'fine'.

"Help would be nice," I reply and feel a flip in my stomach again when Blake smiles at me once more, but it fades when Jack sighs. I tune him out because Blake has taken my arm and walks with me all the way back to the house making sure to take it slow.

"Mom and dad are going to kill me when they get a look at you," Jack says.

"No they aren't. This isn't the first time I've gotten hurt from fooling around. And you aren't to blame."

"You aren't going to tell them it was my fault?"

I look at him like he's crazy, "Do I ever? We don't rat."

He looks relieved.

When we get to the house, I thank Blake softly under my breath and get a nod and smile in return. When we walk inside, Jack starts yelling for our parents and I watch as Blake takes in his surroundings, his eyes roving around our house in every direction.

My mom, who must have returned, comes into the kitchen where we stand and immediately removes the cloth I've been holding at my brow. She starts muttering about crazy kids and stitches. I barely pay her any attention because I'm already thinking about getting to know Blake better. I feel excited about our new neighbor.

I may have been hoping for a young girl my age to be friends with, but something tells me this will be even better.

I had no idea then that I'd end up having a love/hate relationship with that dark haired green-eyed boy, and that he would break my heart over and over again.

2

*J*unior high school is the worst. You would think that dealing with the wonderful world of puberty at this age would be enough, but no. Some of the girls at my stupid school make life a living hell. Not that the boys are any better - they may be worse. It's a toss up. One minute they act like they like you and the next, they ridicule and make fun of you. It's funny because I've heard some of the boys in my grade call the girls "drama" before, but there have been times I'm positive the boys' antics would sell movie tickets. Just give me some popcorn and I'll be set.

High school can't come soon enough - it has to be better, right? I can almost taste how close I am to freedom - I just have to get through this year and then the next and I'll be there.

Jack makes fun of me when he hears me say I can't wait to get to high school. He tells me I'm going to be disappointed, that it will continue to be more of the same. I tell him I can't wait to make new friends and date, but he says girls will still be mean to girls, and that no boy will date me if he has a say.

He's wrong though, on both counts. I know it. Because sometimes it's the only thing that gets me through the bad days.

It won't be long and Jack will be able to give me a first-hand account and let me know if he's right. He and Blake finish junior high this year and go on to high school, leaving me behind. Thinking about it makes my stomach drop and as the year continues to pass quickly, that feeling comes more frequently.

Jack and Blake are simply my best friends. Since the day we met Blake, it's been the three of us - even though there are times Jack wished that weren't the case. Initially, Jack tried to tell me to leave them alone, that just he and Blake were going to play and spend time together. I get it, the last thing he wanted was his little sister hanging around, but the thing is, I didn't have anyone else. Even when Jack was always telling me to get lost, Blake would punch him in the arm, tell him to stop being mean and include me in what-ever they were doing. He never acted like he was tired of me hanging around. When Jack was mean to me, Blake would stick up for me and tell Jack it wasn't a big deal. Eventually, for the most part, at least when we were with Blake, Jack quit trying to get rid of me. And as I grew up there were certainly times I preferred to be alone anyway, but when I did hang out with them, I made it count.

No one was a bigger cheerleader for them than me. When they played video games, needed someone to judge who threw the ball fastest, who's army guy fought best, or to decide who crossed a finish line first, I was their girl. Of course they weren't dumb - there were times they took advantage of the fact they knew I'd do anything just to be included. I lied for them, covered for them, made them food - whatever kept them happy. I figured it was part of paying my dues.

It really came as no surprise when I followed them into junior high and found that they were extremely popular in their class. No doubt when they go on to Mason Creek High it will be the same. Everyone wants to be friends with them, or just be around them. I've seen kids act extremely stupid about it. One time, a boy in my class named Seth was literally run down by Jack as he ran backward to catch a football pass, not bothering to realize that Seth was standing behind him. Seth, who had his back to Jack, couldn't get out of the way fast enough, hit the ground hard, slid and even cut his chin open. For days after, all Seth and his friends could talk about was how Jack was kind enough to help him up and mumble, "Sorry man."

Boys are dumb.

If they knew what Jack looked like when he woke up, how he laughs every time he farts or burps any time he drinks soda, they may think about him differently. Sighing to myself, I roll my eyes, who am I kidding? I'm sure that would just make him rank higher on their cool meter.

I suppose I should be thankful for Jack and Blake's cool status because by association no one messes with me... much. At least not when Jack and Blake are around. No one is that stupid. When they aren't though? Well, then it's open season.

Like today.

Jack and Blake's whole eighth grade class went on a field trip to the history museum. They've been gone all day and I've done my best to ignore the teasing and ridicule that seemed to start as soon as they disappeared on the bus, but it's not easy.

"You're not so tough when your brother and Blake aren't here, are you?" Justin Sanchez, the class bully, says with a cruel laugh. It only gets louder when I look the other way in an effort to ignore him. "Go on, say it. I dare you. Tell me again what you said to me yesterday when I told you that your hair is so gross that you were getting flakes of dandruff all over my desk."

I wish he'd go away and leave me alone. They always say to ignore bullies, that not giving them the attention they want will make them lose interest.

They're wrong. It gets worse.

Justin sits behind me in history class. The whole hour yesterday he kept flicking my ponytail with his finger or pencil. I knew he was just trying to get a reaction, so I tried my best not to give him one. My focus remained on my teacher and I copied notes from Mr. Callahan's teachings from the board into my notebook, but he became incredibly distracting. Algebra isn't my best subject either, so I require all the concentrating and notes possible to help me keep the B I have in that subject.

When Justin wasn't getting a reaction from me by flicking my hair, he started pulling it instead. When that went ignored, he began pinching and poking my exposed neck. Finally, having taken enough abuse, I turned around, gave him a stern look and said, "Leave me alone."

That went over about as well as expected. I actually flinched when he laughed. He continued to torment me adding that he was only doing it because my hair was "gross and flakey and snowing all over his desk."

He was lying just to be jerky. Besides, I have *great* hair.

After a particularly hard pull where I could feel hair snap out of my scalp, I loudly told him, "Stop it, now! That hurt!"

Drawing our teacher's attention, he scolded both of us initially. It continued to happen and we called each other names under our breath, until he pulled hard enough to make me yelp. There was more than a few strands of hair that time. Mr. Callahan busted him, gave him detention, and kicked him out for the rest of class. I was relieved.

But, today is a new day.

Turning to him, I glare, "What's got you acting like a spoiled child again today, Justin? The fact you got detention yesterday, or are mommy and daddy fighting because daddy's drinking too much again? Either way, get over it."

I shouldn't have said it. I knew I shouldn't have. It's not nice to comment on the rumors that run through our small town. My mom would be so disappointed in me, but I can't take it back now. The rumors about Justin's family are infamous.

Seeing his eyes widen in disbelief, I turn back around and do my best to ignore him the rest of class. A feeling of guilt settles in my chest and I know what my mom says is right, kindness goes further than cruelty, but I had trouble finding that kindness within me today. Besides, that great advice from my mom usually comes after Jack and I get into a fight, so does it even really count with someone like Justin?

I decide, no.

It's no surprise that Justin doesn't get over it - not at all. Instead, he continues to harass me all day. It seems wherever I turn, he's there. At lunch, he makes a point of walking by me and sniffing loudly, yelling out, "Eww, why do you smell so bad, Sienna?"

This draws nervous laughs from the super mature classmates around me which only spurs him on further.

As if that's not enough, my ultimate nemesis, Hailey Spellman laughs at Justin's antics like he's the funniest and smartest boy in the whole school. I see right through her and narrow my eyes. Well, at least I see through her now. At one time she had me completely fooled thinking she was actually my friend. We hung out and she even came over to my house a few times. I was a little annoyed when she came over because she wanted to hang out with me, Jack and Blake and not just me. The reason not dawning on me initially.

Until, one day I was in the bathroom stall at school when Hailey walked in with her friends Stephanie and Rebecca. None of them checked to make sure they were alone before Hailey began speaking about how she's excited to hang out at my house that weekend. Stupidly, I smile to myself, also looking forward to hanging out with her and feeling kind of cool because she was talking about it with her friends. The plan was for her to stay the night too - not just come over for a few hours, and I was really excited. I'd never tell her, but it was going to be my first slumber party. I had a whole agenda planned out that included movies, popcorn, pizza, and manicures. I even had our movie selection picked out and planned on asking her which one she wanted to watch beforehand. Thinking I'd walk out and do just that, Stephanie's words stopped me.

"How are you going to stand it?

My brow furrowed in confusion, my fingers paused from turning the lock on the door to step out.

"Like I do every time, duh," Hailey responded. "I smile at her, and toss some attention her way like she's a good little puppy craving attention. It's called acting, Stephanie. I should get an Academy Award."

Stephanie and Rebecca laughed.

"It works every time," Hailey continued to brag.

"You're so evil," Rebecca said.

"Whatever. I'll do anything I have to do. Blake will be my boyfriend. You wait and see."

Clarity removed the rose-colored glasses I was wearing. My excitement for our slumber party scattered like ashes in the wind. It's hard for me to understand how someone could be so cruel. Unshed tears burned my eyes and clogged my throat, but I did my best to swallow them down. Pushing my shoulders back, I flushed the toilet again even though I already had before they walked in. The sound was like thunder clapping in the bathroom, the lock sounded loudly as it turned and I walked out of the stall glaring at all of them on my way to the sink. While I washed my hands, I took great satisfaction in the shocked look on her face. I didn't say a word, there was no reason to.

Needless to say, she never came over that weekend, or any other. Ever since, there's been a seething hatred between us - not that she has any reason to feel that way toward me. I never even told Jack or Blake about it. What was the point? They don't give her the time of day anyway.

Now, Justin and Hailey have appeared to bond in their mutual dislike for me. I do my best to ignore them, gather my lunch and leave. Tears fill my eyes and I hate it. I'm ashamed I've let them bother me. I'm tired of the moments I've spent wiping away a stray tear in secret because of them individually - them picking on me together is bound to be worse.

I don't expect them to get up and follow me out of the lunch room. They walk behind me as I head toward our next class, and poke fun at me.

"Could she act any more like a boy? Hanging out with Jack and Blake - it's like she thinks she is one," Hailey says with a laugh.

Sometimes, when I'm alone and it's quiet and I reflect on

these moments, I wonder if being in the spotlight because I'm friends with Blake and related to Jack is worth it. Not that I can change who I'm related to, but at times I would much rather be left alone and have no one even know who I am.

My thoughts are interrupted when suddenly someone loudly says, "Leave her alone!"

Shocked, I turn around to find the source and I'm surprised to see Vanessa, a girl that I've only spoken to a couple times, has come to my defense.

"Shut up and stay out of it," Justin, the charmer of the ladies that he is, snaps at her.

"You guys need to get a life. You've been bothering her all day and everyone knows you're only doing it because Blake and Jack aren't here. Once they find out, well, let's just say I don't plan on going to your funerals."

I can't help it, I laugh. Not only at her words but at the pure joy of her unexpected defense of me.

"Whatever, Vanessa. Get lost," Hailey replies and she sounds so ridiculously whiny that I can't help it - I laugh harder.

"What are you laughing at?" Hailey seethes. "You're just a pathetic loser that has no friends and spends the whole day alone and lost when her brother and boyfriend aren't here."

"Blake isn't my boyfriend," I reply automatically.

"You just wish he were," Justin sneers. "Thing is, he probably doesn't even know you're a girl, look at you," he says gesturing to me and I do everything I can not to look down at my jeans and plain blue t-shirt. "Even I can't even tell. No one can."

Oh joy, another round of making fun of my appearance. Like they haven't said this before. It doesn't matter though, his words make a wave of heat run over me like a wave, embarrassment instantly burning my cheeks.

"Look how red her face is," Connor, one of Justin's minions, has joined the party.

"That's because it's true," someone else calls; likely one of Hailey's friends.

"Sienna loves Blake," Hailey sing-songs, "Too bad you'll only ever be his best friend's annoying little sister."

Don't react, I instruct myself. It's exactly what she wants.

"God, Hailey, just when I think you can't get more pathetic, you take the cake again. You're just a sad girl that's so insecure she has to make herself feel better by being mean to others. Mommy and daddy still only paying attention to your stellar big sister, Rose? Picking on others to make yourself feel better is so predictable," Vanessa says.

My eyes widen at her words. Everyone knows that Hailey's older sister is the apple of her parents' eye. Straight A's in high school and everyone in town is talking about the college scholarship offers she already has rolling in. Her parents use each and every opportunity to brag about it.

"I think we all know who the real loser is here," Vanessa adds, and before Hailey can respond she turns to Justin, "And you. Talking about Sienna's appearance? Seriously? That's funny coming from you considering your hair is so long and wavy you look like a pretty, pretty, princess from the back."

Before he can retaliate with something scathing our teacher finally walks up to the locked door we've been waiting outside of while having our battle of wits. Mrs. Ripley apologizes as she tries to unlock the door with her hands full and I'm just thankful her appearance stops my torment - at least for now.

Hailey and Justin shove past me into the room, which is

fine. Turning, I face Vanessa, still surprised that she came to my defense. I try to smile, but given my mixed emotions, I'm afraid it's more of a grimace. She doesn't seem to mind because she smiles at me reassuringly and something within me relaxes a little. It feels good to have someone in my corner. Not knowing how to say thank you and feeling more than a little embarrassed at the whole thing, I dart into class and take a seat.

Once class is over and we're dismissed, I leave as fast as I can and make a beeline for the restroom and shut myself into a stall. Taking deep breaths, I do my best to calm myself and push the cruel words spoken earlier from my mind. All during English class they kept replaying in my mind over and over, my insides feeling like the words were actually chewing me up. This time, I can't resist and I do look down at myself. I've got my favorite pair of faded blue jeans on and my blue t-shirt has a character from one of my favorite TV shows on it. I loved it and begged my mom to get it for me when it was at one of my favorite stores in the mall. I guess maybe I do wear it a little too much.

My Vans are also well worn and my hair is in its ever-present ponytail since I prefer it out of my face. I may not be wearing a dress or skirt like some girls, but that doesn't mean I look like a boy.

Hailey and Justin's words cut to the quick because I do have a secret crush on Blake. I have since the day we met, and they're right, I'm only Jack's little sister. Sometimes, I can convince myself that maybe he likes me too. Each time he smiles at me, flicks my ponytail, teases me or winks at me, I feel hope inflate like a balloon in my belly. I want to think it's more than just some young girl's imagination and fantasy.

The bathroom door opens and I realize a few tears fell

down my cheeks. Grabbing toilet paper I wipe them away as my stomach drops, fearful Hailey has found me. Taking a deep breath, I prepare to open the door.

"Sienna?" A soft voice calls.

Relief rushes over me like a cool breeze and I open the door to find Vanessa standing there with a concerned look on her face. "I waited outside the door for you," she gestures toward it, "but got worried," she shrugs.

"Why?"

"Why what?"

"Why are you worried? About me?"

I look closely at Vanessa. I don't see humor twinkling in her eyes or find a hint of a mocking smile on her face. Her light blonde hair is pulled up into a ponytail like mine, but she's got a ribbon tied around it that matches the red dress she's wearing today. She's one of the most mature girls in my class, body wise. It's true, I've found myself wondering a time or two if my boobs will ever get as big as hers already seem to be. Certainly no one would ever mistake *her* for a boy, that's for sure.

She shrugs, "I like you. You're cool. And Hailey and Justin are assholes," she says and a genuine smile comes over my face at the sound of her cursing.

"Yeah, they are," I agree and place my backpack on the floor before I begin washing my hands in the sink. Keeping my focus on them, I add, "You don't have to worry about me though, I can handle myself."

"I know you can, but you don't always have to alone. We can all use a friend sometimes too. I'd like to be yours."

Hesitantly, I raise my eyes to her and again evaluate her face closely. She seems genuine. I've never seen her fawning over Jack or Blake so I don't think this has anything to do with them. In fact, I suppose I haven't really seen her hang out with any particular group of people. She seems to be a bit of a loner too, like me.

"How about tomorrow we sit together at lunch?" She asks me.

"I'd like that," I admit.

"Me too."

We both smile, and with a nod we head out of the bathroom and toward the next class we both share, already late, but I could care less.

The rest of the day is decent, Hailey and Justin get in little digs here and there, but I ignore them. Vanessa and I pass notes back and forth during History class when our teacher isn't looking. Phones aren't allowed in class, so good 'ol paper and pen has to do. We get to know each other, asking things like what our favorite animal is, our favorite celebrity crush, movie, and what food we'd eat the rest of our life if we could only choose one. I had to think for a while on that one.

When school is finally over, Vanessa and I are standing at the front entrance, our phones finally in hand, exchanging numbers. Cars pull in and out picking up students and I wait for Jack and Blake to return because we always take the school bus home together. Vanessa says her mom always picks her up.

We're talking about our last class of the day - our elective drama - and giggling about the fact our teacher had some of her lunch left in her teeth. I tried to tell her - raised my hand to point it out - but she sternly told me it wasn't the time for questions or comments and to pay attention. I decided I didn't care that much about telling her after all and instead tried to hide a laugh when Vanessa looked at me and exaggerated scratching the front of her teeth.

Suddenly, a body slams into my shoulder and knocks my

backpack off my arm. Wincing in pain, I lean down to pick up my bag. "Look, it's Sienna and Vanessa. Together again," Justin's voice rings in the air.

Hailey joins in, "First you defend her, then you hang out the rest of the day, and now you're here. Wow. I didn't know you were into girls, Vanessa."

Feeling my face burn, I pick up my bag and spin to face Justin and Hailey, so tired of their antics. Before I can fire off the words on the tip of my tongue, Vanessa simply rolls her eyes, "Oh, good one. Take you two all afternoon to come up with that one?"

Something about her reaction calms me and I take a cue from her and bravely add, "I'm sure it did, V," I give her a nickname like we've known each other forever. "After all, they do seem to be two peas in a pod today themselves. Like tweedle dee and tweedle dum, emphasis on *dumb*."

Vanessa laughs outright. Shock, humor and something that looks like pride cross her face. As if she's happy I fought back. "It's a toss up which is which, huh Sienna?"

Justin's face instantly screws up in anger and he takes a threatening step toward me until he's in my face and his hands are squeezing the tops of my arms. His grip is so tight, I'm sure he's leaving imprints of his fingers.

"Get off of me!" I shake my arms, but he only grips me tighter.

"You're a stuck up bitch who thinks she's more important than she is. Stay out of my-"

"What the *hell* is going on here?"

I almost sag at the sound of that voice. It's as if the stress and humiliation from the day all release and I suddenly feel heavy. Worn out.

Looking past Justin I see the very, very, angry faces of

Jack and Blake making their way toward us. Jack's hands are clenched at his sides, his eyes angrily stare at Justin's hands.

"Get your hands off my sister. Now."

Justin releases me, but not before giving them once last squeeze which makes me flinch.

"Are you okay?" Blake is immediately at my side and once I nod, he too turns to Justin. Several of Jack and Blake's friends form a wall around us as well, blocking our view from any teachers or parents in vehicles picking up their kids.

"Want to tell me why your hands were on her?" Jack asks. He's so close to Justin's face it's amazing Justin isn't peeing his pants.

"She's been running her mouth all day, man. You know how chicks can be. She and I just needed to sort out a few things. That's all."

"Cut the crap, Justin. You've been on her case all day long tormenting her like crazy. She finally stands up for herself and you act like the victim? I don't think so," Vanessa says and I know I could catch flies with my mouth, as my mom would say. Where has Vanessa been? Why is she just now being my friend? I don't know, but I'm grateful.

I didn't think it was possible for Jack to get any more in Justin's face, but he manages. Justin's face instantly flushes and I feel great satisfaction at seeing that. He tries to step back a step, but Jack only follows.

"Don't ever let us catch you with your hands on her again," Jack says.

"Don't even let us see you looking her way," Blake adds.

"Understood?" Jack asks.

"Y-yes," he nods jerkily.

"That goes for when we're not here too. Don't think for one second that we don't know what goes on when we're not here. Even when we don't go to this school anymore, we'll still know what happens, and we will be here, and we will find you if needed. It would be in your best interest to remember that," Blake adds, his voice full of venom.

Jack pushes Justin away from him after Blake speaks and Justin scrambles away as fast as possible. "Are you sure you're okay?" my brother asks.

"Yeah. Thanks." Turning to Vanessa I smile, "Thank you as well. For everything you did today."

"You don't have to thank me."

Jack and Blake start walking toward the waiting bus, "Come on, Si," Blake calls stopping to wait for me when he sees I'm not immediately following.

"Okay, I'm coming."

I'm stopped in my pursuit by Vanessa's hand on my arm. "Hang out tomorrow too?"

A smile moves over my face like a flower blooming in the sun. "Yeah. I'd like that."

Vanessa and I became almost inseparable after that day. It made the eventual graduation of Blake and Jack into high school easier to handle knowing I wouldn't be alone.

There was also joy in the fact that Vanessa was my friend, for me. It had nothing to do with who my brother and his best friend were. Junior high finally started to not suck after that day.

3

*T*he Valentine's Day cards sitting on my desk mock me. I thought the little cards stating "I'm A Sucker For You" would be cute to pass out to my friends with a lollipop. It's my favorite candy, I almost always have one. Blake teases me about my love for them. One time he took mine out of my mouth and popped it into his own and I almost had an aneurysm. Now a freshman in high school, my major crush on him hasn't let up - if anything it's only worse.

The smile gracing my mouth over that lollipop memory falls off my face in degrees knowing it's silly of me to even let my mind wander to wild or not so wild fantasies. Thinking about it is a certain kind of emotional suicide because my hopes and dreams simply die when my thoughts go to that place. Without a doubt I know that there's no point in fixating, let alone expanding, on my feelings for Blake Walker so I have no idea why my heart continues to betray my mind.

With a sigh I roll over in my bed turning away from the Valentine's on my desk, not wanting to think any more about what my friends have dubbed, 'love day'. Besides, I have plenty of other things to do today. Homework, laundry, a book I'm in the middle of reading - all more productive than the wallowing I've been caught up in.

Unrequited crushes suck, big time.

I've got it so bad for Blake that sometimes it's all I can think about. The feelings twist my stomach, wrench my heart, and frequently leave me breathless. Occasionally it causes me to wonder that if a crush can leave me feeling this way, what will it be like to fall in love? I'm not really sure if I ever want to fall in love because a simple crush is enough to drive me crazy.

My best friend, Vanessa, is the only one that knows about my feelings - although if I'm honest I think my mom may suspect too even though I've never said anything directly to her about it. I do remember the day I confessed my feelings to Vanessa though. I was so nervous, thinking I was divulging a huge secret - and I was as far as I was concerned - but Vanessa laughed. And laughed. Really it was quite rude how long she carried on about it. She told me that she had always known and thought it was funny I actually thought it wasn't as obvious as the nose on my face, or some silly expression like that. It resulted in my totally freaking out, afraid that if she knew then others and Blake had to know too. She assured me that if others suspected, they didn't say gossip about it and that boys aren't nearly as perceptive as girls. I gladly took her word because the thought of anything different was too much to bear.

Thank goodness for Vanessa and her friendship. Life before her was simply boring. She's the only reason that life didn't completely suck when Blake and Jack moved on to high school. Their absence was sharply felt, but I know it would have been far worse without her. Thankfully I never ran into any trouble without them there to come to my defense. The previous bullies seemed to remember Jack and Blake's threats all too well and knew bothering me wasn't worth their ire. And otherwise I just seemed to fade into the woodwork and stay under the radar.

The day I finished my last day of eighth grade I dreamed about setting foot in Mason Creek High. I couldn't wait to be in the same school as my brother and Blake again and to finally feel like I was a regular part of their lives again. Being in separate schools put distance between us that felt like a vast uncrossable canyon. I felt so on the outside of everyday conversations. They'd refer to people and teachers, none of which I had any knowledge about and of course, since I was only in junior high, I wasn't invited to any of their social or sporting events and activities. Well, I got to attend a few games they participated in, but merely as a spectator and typically sitting with my parents or Vanessa. Jack certainly didn't want his little sister trailing along. It sucked.

My first day in high school was even better than I could have ever anticipated. It seemed as soon as I stepped foot onto campus I was instantly popular. Classmates and teachers alike knew who I was, and yeah, it was because I was Jack's little sister and Blake's friend. It was similar to middle school, but even more intense. Everyone either wanted to be friends with them, or simply be them. And why? Well, because they were exactly what every American boy dreams to be – a popular jock. The two of them were basically a football coach's wet dream - they loved the game, were obsessed with working out and kicking ass - and they were realizing amazing results, winning game after game. They were our small town's football heroes - sophomores already playing on the varsity team - and while I loved them to pieces, sometimes I hated it too. Until I managed to find my own way.

Joining the volleyball team sort of happened by accident. We played the game in gym class and I was surprisingly good at it. Our gym teacher also happened to be the coach and she asked me to try out which I did. I loved it, and joining the team helped me establish my own group of friends and reputation in school as a good student and athlete in my own right. The best thing is that they really didn't care about my brother or Blake. Maybe because my teammates are just lowly freshman like me, but regardless Vanessa is really my only trusted friend in the bunch. She never misses a game and has been my biggest support in more ways than one.

Admittedly, I expected Jack and Blake would likely ignore me, too involved in their own friends, the girls that seemed to trail after them like puppies, and football to give me much attention, but I was wrong. They made a point of making me part of their group. They hung out at my locker sometimes, stopped into my class before or after to talk, and sometimes even came and sat down with me at lunch until I'd make them leave me and my friends alone.

Sitting up with a sigh, I catch my reflection in the mirror over my dresser. My dark hair is in disarray and I run my hands through the thick waves trying to bring order. My large blue eyes follow the movements of my hands, trace the lines of my cheekbones and the fullness of my lips before I stare into them and admire my naturally thick lashes. Vanessa curses my luck and tries to emulate them with layer after layer of mascara. My eyes are my best feature I guess, but I hate how expressive they can be. Dad says I'm like my mom, you just have to look into them hard enough to know exactly what I'm thinking. I roll my eyes just thinking about it. My mom is beautiful and people say I look a lot like her, but I don't think I'm attractive really and certainly wouldn't call myself beautiful. I'm not unattractive by any means, and I've been asked out by a couple boys already, but I've turned them all down.

They aren't the one I really wish would ask.

Gathering all my hair into one hand, I raise it to the top of my head and turn my face side to side before letting it all go. Watching it fall around my shoulders I admit to myself that it wouldn't matter if I were the most beautiful girl in the world, Blake wouldn't even notice. All I am, and all I'll ever be to Blake is Jack's little sister.

My phone begins ringing loudly and I jump at the loud sound in my quiet room. Snatching it off my bedside table, surprise raises my brows when I see Blake's name and photo on the screen.

After clearing my throat, I answer, "Hey, Blake. What's up?"

"Hey Si," he says shortening my name which he's done for years. "Are you busy right now?"

"Uh, no, not really. Why? What do you and Jack want?" Usually when one of them calls me it's because they want me to come keep count of their weight reps or something stupid like that. If I didn't enjoy watching Blake's muscles bulge when he lifted I would find it annoying - I'm sure of it.

"It's just me, actually. That needs something I mean," he says and he sounds nervous which makes my stomach clench. This isn't like him.

"Okay..."

"I was wondering if you would come to the store with me? I could really use your help with something."

"Okay, sure. I can help you," I tell him automatically.

"Yeah? You sure you don't mind?"

"I'm sure."

"Sweet. I'll swing by in five. That enough time?"

"Yeah. Yes. Of course. Fine. I'll be ready." Could I sound anymore stupid? You would think I haven't ever spoken to him or hung around him for years.

"Okay, be there soon."

"Okay," I say again and hang up.

Sitting on the edge of my bed, then immediately standing up again, I wonder what in the world he needs my help with? He's never asked me to go to the store with him before. I mean, sure he's taken me for ice cream or given me a ride here or there, but this... something about this feels different.

Realizing I'm wasting time, I look down at myself and gasp. Seeing a small spill on my shirt from breakfast, I strip it off and throw it across the room in the direction of the laundry basket before turning to my closet. Moving hanger after hanger to the side dismissing each shirt I see, my eyes finally land on one of my favorite blue shirts with a cute floral pattern that has straps that cross in the front. It will look fine with the jeans I've already got on.

Pulling it over my head quickly, I shove my feet into some silver flats then grab a sweater just in case. It's mid-February and while the winter has been mild, it can change on a dime so it's best to be prepared.

Ducking into the jack-and-jill style bathroom that I share with Jack who's bedroom is on the other side, I lock his side of the door so he doesn't come in while I make sure my hair is tame and straighten any out-of-place hairs, then grab some lip gloss from the drawer and swipe it across my lips. I grab my cream blush and dab a little color onto my cheeks being careful to keep it natural. I don't want it to look like I tried too hard.

Happy with the result, I unlock Jack's door, leave the bathroom, grab my phone and head to the living room where I immediately look out the window to see if Blake has arrived yet.

My mom looks up from her computer, "Going somewhere?"

"Yeah, Blake is picking me up." Her right brow raises in curiosity. I'm sure its because I only said Blake's name and not Blake and Jack. "He said he needs my help with something at the store," I shrug.

She nods, "Bring your phone," she instructs. Holding it up in my hand so she can see I've already got it, she nods. "Be back within a couple hours for dinner, alright?"

"Okay, I will."

"And tell Blake he can eat with us if he'd like. He hasn't been over for a little while."

We give each other a look and I nod, knowing exactly what she's thinking. The past few years Blake's mom has... changed. Blake's dad walked out on his family and ever since then his mom hasn't been the same. She's developed an unhealthy relationship with alcohol and there's been a few "episodes" that have happened in town. They've been so bad that various business owners in town have had to call Blake to ask him to come and remove his mother - so of course that means the whole town knows. Word travels fast in a small town like ours.

I can't imagine how hard it has to be on Blake and his sister. I've overheard Jack talking to our parents about it, but they usually found me snooping and I wasn't privy to much of the conversation. I've still heard the things people have whispered about at school though, never daring to say anything to his face. It's sad and I know it's taking a toll on him. He's extremely somber at times; stressed. At times he looks like he's carrying the weight of the world on his shoulders.

Doing my best, I try to shake the thoughts from my mind. I don't want to be transparent or somber when Blake picks me up. He has a sixth sense for when something is bothering me and it's weird he can be so intuitive about some things and completely clueless about others.

Checking outside once more, I see his old red pickup truck pulling up into our driveway.

"He's here. I'll be back soon."

"Okay," my mom says absently, her attention back to whatever she's looking at on her computer. "Seatbelt," she calls out as an afterthought.

"Always," I reply as I close the front door behind me.

Blake's just closed the door to his truck when he catches sight of me, "Hey," he smiles, "I was just on my way to the door."

"I saw you pull up." He walks around the truck and opens the passenger door for me. Once I climb up inside, I buckle my seatbelt as promised and watch as he climbs in and does the same.

He starts the truck again with a look at me and smiles. Jack smiling is a gift by itself. When he does, his eyes light up, and as his mouth lifts in the corners, crinkles appear at the edges of his eyes. I love them, and the sight always makes my heart pound a little harder and my lips automatically lift to return the gesture. He turns back to stare out the windshield as he drives and I notice his dark hair is standing on end like he just ran his hands through it and that's where the strands ended up. He has a nervous habit of doing that when he's stressed and I can't help but wonder what's making him feel on edge. My face falls when I wonder if there's trouble with his mom again.

"Are you okay?" Blake asks.

"Me?" I ask surprised. "Yeah, why?"

"You just looked sad for a minute. Your whole face seemed to change."

"Oh. No. I'm fine," I say forcing a smile.

"Thanks for coming with me."

"Sure! But, what are we going to the store for?" I ask curiously.

"Actually, we're going to make a quick run to the mall. I need your help picking something out for someone."

"Alright," I respond expecting he'll tell me what we're looking for exactly, but he doesn't.

"How's school been going lately? I haven't really talked to you one on one in a while. I assume if anything was going on, Jack would have said, but I should still check in more often."

"No, it's ok. Everything is fine, there's nothing to report," I shrug. "I guess I'm pretty boring."

He smirks, "There's nothing boring about you, Si."

My breath catches, but somehow I manage to say, "I can't believe we're already in the fourth quarter. It won't be long and it will be summer break."

"I'm *so* ready for that."

"Why? School not going great for you?" I ask with clear doubt in my voice. "I mean, don't get me wrong, I can't wait for summer either. I guess I just figured our school's wonder boy would be dreading the end."

"Wonder boy?"

Smiling I shrug, "You heard correctly."

He shakes his head looking amused, but then sobers. "School is fine, I guess. Things have just been... stressful... at home. I think it will be good when I can spend more time there and not have to worry about school."

"Oh," I stay quietly feeling bad knowing why he's saying that. Hesitantly I ask, "What's going on?"

He doesn't answer right away. The silence is long enough to make me wonder if I made a mistake asking and he's just going to pretend I didn't. "My mom has been drinking a lot," he confesses suddenly and I still. "It started casually. A glass of wine at home after a stressful day. A few drinks when she went out with friends after working all day. Eventually it became every day and more than one to 'unwind'."

"Oh man, I'm sorry. No wonder you're feeling stressed."

"Yeah," he takes the opportunity while we're stopped at a stoplight to run his hand through his hair. "It's only a matter of time until she gets fired. She's missed too many days and then showed up at work drunk a couple weeks ago. They called me and asked me to come get her. Mr. Kimble had empathy for her I guess because he didn't toss her out for good that day but did tell her to get herself together, but I'm already expecting it's coming."

"That didn't make her stop? Realizing that she's going to lose her job?"

He laughs without humor, "No. It seems to have only made her drink more. I think I'll have to get a job to help support us."

"How are you going to do that, Blake? You have school. And when school is over, sports. And sports camps."

"I'll figure it out," he shrugs. "She's already the talk of town. I imagine someplace will take pity on me and give me a job knowing why I need one."

"Sometimes I hate living in a small town."

"Yeah," he nods. "At least no one at school has said anything to me about it."

"They wouldn't dare," I shake my head at the thought of someone being so stupid.

"Yeah, I suppose you're right. I'd likely kick them in the

teeth," he laughs. "But sometimes I'm surprised one of the counselors haven't taken me aside to make sure I'm ok...you know given that my dad's gone."

"Yeah, I get it," I nod. "How's Mandy doing with all of this," I ask about his sister.

"She's counting down the minutes until she graduates and," he uses air quotes, "gets the hell out of this town. I can't really blame her. She and my mom argue all the time. Mandy's angry. Angry at my dad, angry at my mom. I get it. I just don't see the point in acting out the way she does. How does that help?"

"I'm sorry," I say again at a loss for what else I should say. "It has to be hard to watch."

"It is," he nods. "We tried you know? Every time she would bring bottles home, when we realized it was a problem, we'd dump them out. Hide them. Whatever we needed to do. It didn't take long though before she would hide it too."

"Oh no."

"I read that it's typical behavior. When we would dump it and get rid of it, she'd rant and rage at us. We thought for a time she was getting better, but eventually we just realized she was hiding vodka in her water bottles, in other liquids, I even found a bottle of tequila under the bathroom sink once. Fact is, if someone wants to do something, they'll find a way. It doesn't matter how much you try to stop it. I finally realized that I can't make her stop. She has to decide that for herself."

"That has to make you feel helpless."

"It does. I just don't understand why you would choose to live your life like that."

I just nod, knowing I don't have the words that can make any of it better. Instinctively I know that he just needs to talk to someone. I can't really picture him venting all of this to Jack. I imagine their conversations center more around how many reps they did when they worked out, what they should eat and of course which girl's ass is the nicest. They are guys after all.

"I hardly even recognize my mom anymore," he confesses. "It's sad. But sometimes, I get glimpses of her and I refuse to give up on her yet."

"Do you have some family you can call to help? Does she have siblings? Your grandparents? You shouldn't have to take all of this on yourself. And you know, a school counselor may be able to give some advice or point you in a direction where support would be available for you and Mandy."

"There's no one," he says with such finality I don't ask any questions or make suggestions. Instead, I sit in silence as we finally pull into the mall parking lot and Blake searches for a place to park.

Once we head inside, I finally ask, "So, spill it. What do you need my help buying? Is Mandy's birthday coming up?"

He smiles and something about it looks shy, "No. It's not for Mandy."

"Then who?" I ask curiously. I know I'm not crazy when I see Blake's cheeks flush with a little color. "Blake?" I ask again, the sight surprising. Who knew Blake could get embarrassed about anything?

"I... well..." he hesitates and I don't know why, but the little hairs on my arms raise with goosebumps. "I need your help picking out a Valentine's Day gift for... someone."

My stomach drops and I instantly feel sick. Saliva gathers in my mouth and I swallow several times before I manage to utter, "Someone?"

"Yeah," he replies.

"Who?" I ask and I know that one word was several octaves high.

He looks into my eyes, then looks away. "I don't want to say...yet. I just want your honest unbiased opinion. Plus, I'm just no good at this kind of thing and I don't want to screw it up. I want it to be... special."

Yep. I'm going to throw up. My eyes dart around looking for a bathroom.

"I'll tell you about her though."

Somehow I manage to nod.

"I've known her... for a long time. One day, I just... I don't know... saw her differently."

My brows lower, "Differently?"

"Yeah, differently. You know, in the way guys like girls."

"Well obviously, I guess I just mean, what changed?"

"I don't really know. I never let my thoughts or emotions even go in that direction before. It wouldn't have been right. But then, one day, it just slammed into me. I realized I like her, a lot. I think maybe I have for a while. I fought it though, really hard. I didn't feel right about it."

"How come?" I ask trying to sound casual when what I really want to do is scream at him demanding answers.

"Because being with her will make someone... well a few people maybe... very unhappy." He looks in my eyes again, before looking away.

"I don't understand."

"I know Jack is one. He's not going to be very happy with me."

A small flame of hope ignites in my heart and my breath catches in my throat, but I push past it, afraid to let myself hope.

"Can you tell me something about her?" I ask him desperate for a sign. Any freaking sign.

He runs his hand through his hair, "Well, like I said, I've known her awhile, but she's younger than me," he pauses. "She loves animals, reading, and listening to music."

I can't help but think that these are all things that I like too. The flame inside of me flickers higher.

"What I think is really cool is that she's totally like one of the guys sometimes."

It takes everything inside of me not to scream my head off. It's me. It has to be me. I mean, I hang out with him and Jack all the time. I have more books in my room than anything else, clearly I'm sporty and love taking care of all the animals on my farm. It's me. How can it not be? Oh my god.

"She sounds... nice," I manage to say casually like it's just any other day and this is any other moment.

He smiles at me, meeting my eyes once more, before looking away again. He's acting so shy and it's adorable. Would turning to him and saying, 'I like you too!' be too much? What would he do? What will I do? Jump into his arms. Oh my god, what if he wants to kiss me? Does my breath smell okay? I blow into my hand and smell just to be sure.

"She is. So, you'll help me?"

"Yeah," I smile at him, the worry inside from before completely sated, excitement and wonder taking its place. "I'd be happy to."

"Any ideas?"

I smile widely, "I've got a few."

A couple hours later, Jack and I are back in his truck headed back to my place. A bright red gift bag sits between us and I can't stop stealing glances at Blake, wondering how exactly he's going to give me the gift I picked out - for myself. What will he say? How will he tell me it was me he was talking about the whole time? Will he talk to me privately? Give it to me at my locker?

When we pull up to my house, Blake parks and turns to me with a big smile, "Thank you, again. I know that she will love the gift you picked out," he laughs softly and it just seems like he's playing a fun game with me now.

"I'm sure she will. I know she will actually," I confess.

"I enjoyed spending some one on one time with you, Sienna. Its been a while. I look forward to doing it again, soon."

I can't keep the wide smile from my face if I tried. "Me too."

Hopping out of the truck, I close the door, give Blake a wave and go to the front door. I can't help but look over my shoulder back at him to find him watching me. Turning away, I know I have to immediately figure out what I'm going to wear to school tomorrow, and of course call Vanessa to tell her everything that just happened so we can dissect every single word spoken.

The next morning, I'm nervous as I walk into school. I took the time to curl my hair and the curls falling down my back, combined with the extra time I took to apply a little more makeup that I usually wear make me feel pretty. Jack made fun of me when I walked out of my room this morning teasing me about it being Valentine's Day and asking me if I think I'll have anyone ask me if I'll be their Valentine today. He laughed at himself like it was the funniest joke, but I'm not about to let him ruin today for me. He can keep his opinion to himself. I don't care what he thinks about this.

When I get to my locker, I'm surprised Vanessa is there already, that girl is almost always late. "There you are," she says when she sees me.

"Hey," I tell her while I quickly place my bag into my locker once I get it open and then smooth my hands down my shirt. "What are you doing here already?"

"Miracles happen."

I laugh, "Do I look okay?" I ask her, vulnerability clear in my voice."

She stills and smiles at me, "You look great, Sienna. You always do."

"Thanks, I'm nervous."

"Sienna-"

"When do you think I'll see him? Do you think he'll take me aside? Give me the gift here at school? Maybe wait until afterward?"

"Sienna-"

"I mean, if he's worried about Jack seeing, he may want to wait. Which will drive me crazy all day, but I understand."

"Sienna," she says more firmly and grabs my hand. "Listen to me."

Really looking at her for the first time since I arrived, I see that she seems upset.

"What's wrong?"

She hesitates and something inside of me twists sharply.

"Just tell me."

"The gift isn't for you."

I look at her with clear confusion. There's sadness in her eyes, she's squeezing my hand and she looks nervous. I laugh, "What do you mean? How do you know? Of course-"

She looks over her shoulder, then back at me, "Look down the hall."

Frowning, my eyes move away from her and down the hallway. There's a small crowd of people and I'm not sure at first what's got people's attention, but then I realize it isn't what - it's whom.

Trying to look through the crowd to see what's going on, it suddenly parts and I see what's got everyone curious. Blake is standing there, and wrapped around him like an octopus in heat is none other than Hailey Spellman.

I wait. I wait for him to push her off. I look at Vanessa and again see the concern on her face. Looking back down the hall again, I shake my head as if doing so will make what I"m seeing go away.

"I don't understand. Vanessa," I plead as if she has all the answers. Instead I just repeat, "I don't understand."

"I got here early. I wanted to see Blake talk to you. I saw-" my eyes swing back to her and she hesitates for a moment before saying, "I saw him give her a red bag. I saw him give her the gift. I'm so sorry."

"But, that can't be right. He was talking about me. I'm sure of it. Wasn't he?"

In a cruel twist of fate, Blake's head turns in my direction and he makes eye contact with me. I watch as he says something to Hailey, and she nods letting go of him. Blake begins walking to me and since I can't stop looking between the two of them in shock, I don't miss Hailey's eyes finding mine. I watch as she reaches up to her neck and tugs on the silver chain around her neck that I know has a small dainty silver heart hanging from it. Because I just helped Blake pick it out the day before.

"Oh my god," I whisper quietly.

Hailey, well, she can probably see my feelings all over my face. Because she does something that if I didn't already hate her, I surely would now.

She smirks at me.

Smirks. At. Me.

"What a bitch," Vanessa says in defense of me and I

almost laugh. Almost. But I'm sure it would sound hysterical and crazed.

Blake reaches me and it takes me a minute to realize he's speaking, "So thank you."

"Wh-what?" I ask in confusion. All I hear is a ringing in my ears.

Blake's brows furrow, "I said, thank you for your help picking out the gift. Hailey loves it. And I know this is a surprise, I don't want you to be mad about this. I know how you feel about Hailey, but she's not as bad as you think, okay? We'll talk soon, alright? I promise."

He waits for me to answer and I manage a nod.

He smiles and begins walking back to Hailey. I feel Vanessa's hand on my arm subtly offering comfort and I do my best to keep the burn behind my eyes at bay.

"Let's go to the bathroom," Vanessa whispers.

"Y-yes." I nod and allow Vanessa to lead me away.

"Oh, hey, Sienna?" Blake calls out and I look over my shoulder. "Happy Valentine's Day."

He turns around and makes his way back to Hailey, puts his arm around her shoulders, and smiles at her.

He gives her *my* smile.

He gave her *my* necklace.

He gives her *my* heart.

Watching it, feels unbearable, and my heart breaks into a million tiny pieces.

4

_S_itting on Vanessa's bed watching her curl her hair into waves down her back, I'm second guessing our plans this evening. I'm not sure why I let her talk me into things I'm not sure I want to do. Yes I do, because she's more fun than I am.

"I don't understand how you can even be questioning whether or not you should go," she points the curling iron at me in irritation. "It's not even a choice, really, because everyone's going," she tells me for the third time in less than an hour. "_Everyone._"

And I tell _her_ for the third time in less than an hour, "Just because everyone is going, doesn't mean I have to."

She doesn't even try to hide her annoyance with me. I decided long ago she could win an Olympic medal in eye-rolling if they had one. The thought makes me smirk in amusement. "What would you do instead?"

I shrug my shoulders.

"I know what you would do. You'd sit in your room, sulk, maybe read something, but most likely you'd write your sad feelings in your diary."

"Yeah, so? Maybe I would. I don't know."

"I do. It would be something like... dear diary, it's another day in the life of my unrequited love obsession with Blake. Oh diary, why for art thou doth he not love me?" She places the curling iron down so she can put the back of her hand to her forehead for dramatic effect.

"Stop it. That doesn't even make sense," I laugh at her theatrics.

"Seriously, Sienna, stop questioning whether or not you're going. You're going. Best friends don't let best friends miss parties like this. It's my duty to make sure you're there."

"Your duty?"

"Yep," she says with a whole lot of sass. "Now get over here, it's your turn."

With a sigh I get up and walk over to her and she immediately starts brushing my hair while still lecturing me, "It's a few months until the end of the school year, and we deserve to let go and let loose for once. We've been working hard all year long."

I mean, she's not wrong about that. I've thrown myself into my studies because it's prevented me from thinking about...other things.

"Plus, you look hot. Like capital H-O-T, hot. I couldn't have picked a better outfit for you myself. You can't back out now, why are you trying to?"

I mean, I guess she's not wrong. I look at myself closely in the mirror while she separates my hair into sections before curling them. I took great care doing my makeup, in part because it's something I love to do. My allowance usually goes to the latest must-have makeup product I read about and I'm acquiring quite the collection. I chose my new white jeans that fit me like a glove which I miraculously convinced my mom to buy for me. To go with them, I'm wearing a cute floral top found at one of my favorite boutiques when we went shopping out of town. It shows just a hint of my boobs and I know I look good. But whether or not I look good isn't the problem. My heart just isn't in this tonight.

And I know why.

Blake and Hailey.

It's been a few months since Valentine's Day officially became the stupidest holiday ever. And the reason for that is still going strong. Unfortunately. And I do everything I can to avoid them. It makes me sad. I miss my friend. Blake's noticed the distance too. Whenever he's at the house hanging out with Jack and I'm around, he makes a comment about how he never sees me anymore. Usually I just shrug, smile like I'm sorry, and make an excuse to be somewhere else. My excuses range from 'I'm meeting up with Vanessa', to 'I have so much homework to do', or 'I've got a horrible headache and need to lay down'. I rarely have dinner with the family when he joins. I'm positive my mom knows that I'm struggling. She tried to bring it up once and I completely shut her down. She hasn't tried to broach the subject since, but she gives me these I-know-what-you're-doing eyes which I ignore.

Plain and simple, I don't have the energy to fake it within me, so I avoid, avoid, avoid. I just don't get it - he betrayed me. How can he be with a person that made my life hell? He was my friend first - does he not have any loyalty? Apparently if you have a pair of double d's and there's rumors that you know how to use your big lips, that's all that matters.

Gross.

Finally, I decide to just say what I'm thinking, "You know why I don't want to go, but if you need me to say it, fine. I'm pretty sure Blake and Hailey will be there and I don't really want a front and center seat to the Blake and Hailey show."

"I get it, Sienna," I give her a how could you possibly understand look, but she shakes her head. "Stop. I do understand, but enough is enough. You don't just stop living your own life because he's choosing to hang out with someone you don't like. The best way to get over him, is to get with someone else."

"You make that sound so bad."

"I'm not telling you to slut it up, I'm telling you to stop putting your own life on pause in the hopes that Blake comes to his senses. Fact is, he may never. You have guys that have asked you out repeatedly and you shut them all down. All I'm saying is maybe, I don't know, say yes for once. Just go for it," she shrugs, "What have you got to lose?"

"Nothing," I admit. "Maybe you're right."

"You know I am. And you know what?" She pulls the final curl through the wand and turns it off and unplugs it before facing me.

"What?"

"Todd's going to be there," she says with a small smile.

Todd Masters.

He and I sit next to each other in chemistry class and the boy has been asking me out for weeks. One day, he whispered my name to get my attention even though we sit next to each other. I turned to him and he said, "Did you know that chemists do it on the table periodically?" He wagged his eyebrows up and down and it was so stupid and unexpected, I laughed. And every once in a while since, he has a new joke or one-liner for me. The most recent was, "Hey baby, I've got my ion you. Ion. I-O-N. Get it?" I laughed at his excitement and he winked at me. It's stupid and cheesy, but he got my attention which I know was his objective.

He's not a bad looking guy. Sandy brown hair, hazel eyes, a strong jaw and the body built to match his reputation as one of the top performing and most popular football players in our school. It's obvious he spends a lot of time working out because he's a show stopper.

His jokes morphed into him asking me if I was going to go watch the football game earlier in the year, to then straight out asking me to go so I could watch him. When the season was over he attended a few of my volleyball games and then he just flat out told me we should hang out some time. I mumbled sure, but never really took him up on it and he never pushed. But, as these things go, a girl named Amanda told Vanessa in Spanish class that she had heard from Rory in her public speaking class that Todd was heard telling someone that he likes me. Vanessa has been pushing me toward Todd ever since.

"I think it's way past time you take a ride on that train, if you know what I mean," Vanessa smiles wickedly and I can't help it - I laugh.

"Why do you have to make it sound so dirty?"

She just shrugs and laughs it off, "Seriously, Sienna. Prom is just around the corner and I know you want a date. Let's just go have fun okay?"

Well, she's not wrong. I don't want to be the only junior at prom without a date. She's got a point, but nerves make my stomach feel jittery.

I guess that's why a few hours later, I'm standing in the living room of Max Williams' house drinking my third cup of some concoction a bunch of guys mixed together. They dubbed it "To the Max" after Max's party and everyone has been downing glass after glass. All I know is it's making me brave.

Really brave.

Brave enough that I'm literally standing here flirting with Todd like I have all the experience in the world at being flirtatious. I don't. But apparently I'm doing it well because he's hanging on every word I say.

"I don't know if I really care where I go to college, as long as it's not here. I just want to get out of this town, you know?" I answer him and then laugh and say, "Oops," when I realize some of my drink sloshed over the side of my cup as I gestured.

"I want to go play ball. I don't care where it is either as long as they want to give me a scholarship to play. I've already got interest from University of Montana and Montana State. I plan on going wherever I get the most money," he says,

We're sitting side by side on the long part of a lounge chair next to the pool. We've turned it so we can face everyone and are watching people's antics as we talk. He's just given me another drink that I'm taking gulps of in an attempt to drink as fast as possible because it doesn't taste the greatest. He said it's from a 'special stash'. I don't like it as much as the juice concoction I was drinking before.

The music is so loud, he's leaning into my side and speaking into my ear to be heard. At times his lips brush against my ear and it sends tingles up and down my arms. Maybe I'm into this. My body seems to be more and more.

Across from the pool, Blake sits in a chair too. He's surrounded by his friends, including my brother, and Hailey is all over him. Sometimes she dances in front of him, against him, or like now she sits on his lap draped over him like a blanket. Occasionally he makes eye contact with me, and it's really awkward. He keeps looking from me to Todd and back. I'm avoiding him at all costs as per usual these days, but something about my conversation really seems to be interesting to him if I'm reading him correctly.

"How come you never come to parties?"

"How do you know I don't?" I ask still being flirtatious.

"Because I pay attention."

"Is that code for, you look for me?"

"I've kept an eye out for you," he smiles.

"It's not usually my scene I guess." I find that I'm rather enjoying how I'm feeling right now. My stress and worries seem to have disappeared and my neck feels loose - like my head is floating above it. I could easily just let it fall back, close my eyes, and drift off.

A couple times when Todd has said something funny, I feel like maybe I'm laughing too loud, but if I am, he doesn't seem to mind. I stop worrying about it.

"Why is it your scene tonight?"

"Vanessa made me," I confess. "She says I'm due for some fun. Where even is she anyway?" I ask realizing I haven't seen her in a while.

Todd's eyes fill with mirth and he points. Following his finger, I see Vanessa pressed up against the wall of what I heard was the pool house. There's a guy talking to her, and he's standing very close. She must like it because she's got a smile on her face and I see her laugh from here.

"Who's she talking to?"

"T-bone," Todd says, referring to one of his teammates. "Good for him. He's liked her for a while."

"He has?" I ask, eyes wide with surprise. I've never heard anything about it which is surprising considering people at school can't keep anything quiet.

He nods and smiles and his eyes crinkle in the corners. I've never noticed that before - it's cute. He leans toward me,

"Can I tell you a secret?" He may think he's whispering, but he's not.

"Sure."

"I know someone else who has a crush."

"Oh well, do tell."

"You have to do something for me first."

"What's that?"

"Tell me your plans for the summer."

"Like... what I'm doing?" I ask taken off guard.

"Yeah."

"Well, I'm hoping to get a summer job. I'm hoping to save for college."

"What else?"

"Um, normal stuff I guess. Taking care of the animals on our farm. Hanging out with V."

"Wrong answer," he smirks.

"What do you mean?"

"The correct answer is that you're going to hang out with me."

"Is that right?"

"Yep. That's right. Do you want to know why?"

"Sure, why not? Tell me."

"Because *you* have a crush on *me*."

"Excuse me?" I ask with a surprised laugh.

"It's true," he shrugs

"Is it?"

"Yep."

"You sound awfully confident, especially when I didn't even know that about myself."

"I am. And I know why you do."

"Well, why stop now? Please continue," I smile enjoying our banter.

"It's because of the sweet pick-up lines I've thrown at you all year."

"Oh I see. And you think those were so great that I'm into you now?"

"Well, if not, you will be."

"Yeah? How do you know that?"

He grins and before I can say another word, he leans toward me and puts his mouth on mine. For a moment, I'm taken off guard, surprised because I've never been kissed before. Before I can be insecure and worry if I'm doing this right, his tongue is in my mouth so all I can do is react. I meet his kiss move for move. His arm finds its way around my waist. I clutch one of his upper arms. I am clearly amazing at this. Go. Me. I slide my hand up to his shoulder and-

"Hey!" I holler when I suddenly find myself pulled away from Todd and am face to face with Blake. I wobble on my feet for a moment and he grips both of my arms, steadying me.

"What are you doing?" He asks me, eyes fierce and fiery.

"Excuse me?" I stumble over those two words, feeling confused.

"I asked what you're doing?"

"Um, I'm pretty sure you don't need me to spell it out for you," I giggle because I'm also funny. I'm a good kisser, *and* I'm funny. Score! I'm clearly a catch.

"I think I should bring you home, Si," he says softly.

"What?" I ask pulling away from his hold. "No."

"Yes." He reaches for me again. "You're barely able to stand up straight. How much have you had to drink?"

I don't know what sets me off. Maybe it's the look on his face - like he's disgusted with me. Maybe it's because he's acting like he has the right to be reprimanding me in front of others. Or maybe it's because I was finally not thinking about him for once in... forever... and then he had to mess that up by forcing this interaction. Who in the hell does he think he is?

"What's it to you?" I ask him angrily.

"Come on, I think you've had enough. It's time to call it a night.."

"Really, Blake? Where do you get off telling me what to do? Jack isn't even worried about me. Where even is-" I stop talking when I catch sight of my brother. He's got a girl in his lap and he's eating her face. That's something I never, ever, ever needed to see. "Ew. Never mind. Could have gone my whole life without seeing that," I say.

"It's fine. I don't mind taking care of you. Jack's busy."

"Well news flash, Blake. I don't *need* you to take care of me, okay? How about that? Here's an idea for you," I point at his stupid girlfriend, "Go back and take care of Hailey. Like I said, I don't need you. I am not your concern and none of this is your business."

"Yes you are; come on, let's get Vanessa and we'll go-"

"No!" I say loudly. "I'm not your little sister. I can make my own choices. You aren't responsible for me, okay? You have clearly shown that you don't care about me or want me."

"Sienna-" he says my name a look of shock on his face and it takes me a moment to even realize what I said. I'm spared any embarrassment by Todd's interruption.

"You okay, Sienna?" He asks staring at Blake. Blake glares at him and I'm surprised Todd doesn't back down because Blake's look is harsh enough to stun anyone speechless.

Pulling away from Blake, I grab Todd's arm, "I'm fine. Let's go," I drag Todd past Blake, ignoring his calling my name and move through the crowd. Before I know it, I'm no longer leading Todd, he's leading me. We go down a hallway and take a right to another hall. How big is this house anyway? Eventually he opens a door, looks inside, then pulls me in when he finds it empty.

"It's just you and me again," he says.

I smile, my head feeling even more floaty after all that walking.

"Where were we?" He asks and I don't even get a chance to reply before he's kissing me again.

It feels nice.

His hands move up to my upper arms, and he grabs hold of them while his lips move against mine.

He clearly finds me attractive. He clearly wants me. He may not be my first choice - no - I'm not going there.

He moves me backward and I trip over my own feet. He steadies me and keeps me moving until the back of my legs hit a bed. He pushes me, and I fall backward. His face a blurry smile.

"I don't feel so great," I mumble.

"It's okay. I'm going to make you feel better," he says.

Blake's body is on mine. Wait. No. Not Blake. Todd. Todd's body is on mine. He's kissing me again. Harder this time.

"Ouch," I say and pull back when I feel his teeth bite my lip.

"You like that?" he asks.

Before I can tell him no, his body presses hard against mine. I'm pressed so firmly into the bed, I feel trapped underneath him.

His mouth moves from my mouth, to my neck. I feel his hand move down the front of me, over my breast, to the edge of my shirt before he dives under it and up, squeezing my breast hard.

His hips begin grinding against mine.

I feel like I can't breathe.

The world feels fuzzy.

My reactions feel, slow; like I'm moving through oil.

"No," I mumble.

"Yeah it feels good," Todd says and squeezes me again. "I'm going to make you feel good."

He fumbles with the button of my jeans, pulls the zipper down.

"No," I manage to say again.

I can feel panic rising in my chest. Why can't I tell him how I feel? Why do my arms and legs suddenly feel detached.

"Just lay there. That's right. I'll do all the work."

"No!" I manage to yell and force my head to the side. I feel a sharp pain at my neck and tears come to my eyes. I think he bit me. "Stop," I say again, loudly.

"Stop it, bitch. You've been playing hard to get for months. I know you want it. Stop playing."

"Jack!" I yell helplessly for my brother. "Blake!" I try calling him too, desperate for help.

Someone.

Anyone.

I refuse to stop fighting. I try again to push him off.

"Stop! No!"

Suddenly, I feel empty space. A breeze feels like it slides over my body, as Todd disappears.

I hear, "What the fuck? Get off of her! She said, stop!"

"Blake?" I hear his voice. I know he's there. The tears fall faster now. I can't even sit up.

I hear grunts, flesh hitting flesh, more grunts, then silence.

"I'm here," Blake says, "I'm here." His hands frame my face, "Sienna?"

"I told him to stop," I whisper. "Why can't I move? What's wrong with me?"

He doesn't say a word, but I realize he's straightening my shirt and my pants, then picks me up in his arms.

He carries me out of the room, through the house, and outside, all the while tears continue to fall. I feel stupid, confused and embarrassed. How did this get out of control so fast?

I hear the familiar beep of his truck as he disarms it and he somehow manages to open the door and place me inside.

"I'll be right back."

Fear grips me, and I manage to grab his arm, "Don't leave me."

"I'm not," I can see his face clearly in front of mine. His eyes are soft, familiar, full of worry and... something, "Give me one second."

He shuts the door. I hear his steps disappear, but it doesn't seem like he's gone long. I hear voices, it sounds like arguing because I hear anger. I can make out the murmur of Blake's voice, but nothing clearly. Soon, he's back in the truck.

"Here," he has a bottle of water to my lips. "Drink some of this." I comply. When I'm finished, he places the cap back on the bottle. He doesn't start the car and I roll my head toward him. He's sitting still, his breaths coming harshly. His hands grip the steering wheel and his head is bowed.

"Blake?"

"I just need a minute," he murmurs. "God, Sienna, if I had been just a couple minutes longer..."

Shivers go up and down my spine. "I'm sorry. I'm so sorry," I feel horrible and feel like my words are coming out in slurs.

I know they made sense when he tells me, "Do not apologize. This isn't your fault."

"I drank too much."

"Yes, but I also think Todd put something in your drink."

"What do you mean?"

"Yeah, you drank a lot, but not so much that you should barely be able to move."

Just the thought of drinking now makes me want to be sick.

He finally starts the truck and begins to drive in silence. It takes me a moment before I freak out, cry, and begin to stutter, "I-I-I c-can't go home. M-m-mom and dad - spending night V-Vanessa."

He knows what I'm saying.

"We are going to my house. Mom is working. I'll get you home tomorrow. Now just relax if you can."

When we get to his house, he turns off the truck and comes to my side. He helps me out of the truck and I try to pull away. His arm around me, his care and concern is making me feel things I know I shouldn't even in my pathetic state. He's just being kind - like a brother - *always* like a brother.

"I'm fine. I can walk now. I think the water helped."

"No, I'm helping."

"Actually, maybe you should just take me home. I-I'll come up with some excuse. You don't have to take care of me. Thank you for your help but-"

"Sienna, stop. You're drunk, maybe drugged, I've got you."

"Really, I'm-"

That's as far as I get before projectile vomit gushes without warning. All over Blake's shoes. All over the ground and all over myself. I feel much too horrible to feel embarrassed.

Without a word he helps me inside, takes me straight to the bathroom connected to his bedroom and eases me down to the toilet. He spends the rest of the evening holding my hair back, pressing cold compresses to the back of my neck, giving me sips of water. He alternates between whispering soothing words of comfort one moment, then promises to kick Todd's ass and make him pay for what he did the next.

Eventually, I begin to feel better. Blake gives me a t-shirt of his to change into and leaves the bathroom while I peel my soiled clothes off of my body. Pulling the shirt over my head, I can't help but draw the fabric to my nose and inhale his scent. Opening the door, I stand there a moment, feeling awkward. Blake's immediately at my side, "Are you okay?"

I simply nod.

He pulls the blankets back on his bed, "Here, get in. Get some rest."

I do as I'm told, too exhausted to do anything else. Blake pulls the covers over me and I watch as he lays down next to me, on top of the covers. He puts his arm over his eyes, and for a while I watch his chest rise and fall, the action relaxing me. I feel safe and I allow the security he provides, plus the scent of him that surrounds me, lull me to sleep.

5

*L*ooking yet again at my prom date, I'm fairly certain I'll have the hottest one of the night - without question.

It's no surprise that not long ago after what was supposed to be a fun night of letting go turned into a nightmare, that prom didn't sound like a good idea to me. Vanessa insisted that there was no way in hell she was going to let me miss my junior prom. She said something about best friends not letting best friends miss prom, but really, she says that any time I don't want to do something. I told her it's starting to lose effectiveness which she promptly ignored.

Considering the fact I'm currently standing in my room wearing a floor length sequin prom dress, I suppose she has more influence on me than I give her credit.

I shudder slightly reflecting on that night and the aftermath. Todd showed up at school the following week with several black and blue areas on his face. He could not conceal the fact that he had been pummeled, mercilessly. Just glancing at him made my own face hurt.

Blake and Jack never admitted to a thing, but I know, hell everyone knows, that they beat the shit out of him. At first, feeling ridiculously stupid and embarrassed, I was adamant the whole situation be kept quiet. Then, Jack had a serious talk with me about his feelings.

The thing about my brother is that he doesn't get that serious often, so when he does, I pay attention. His thoughts were that it was likely I wasn't the only girl that had ever been drugged by Todd or the only one that he had taken advantage of and he suspected that some girls had not been as "lucky" as me. He said my speaking up could potentially save someone else.

I'm ashamed to say my first reaction was anger at Blake for even telling Jack what happened. Blake had to though - he actually had the forethought that night to ask Jack to make sure Vanessa got home safely and to let him know he was taking care of me and why. He knew Jack would likely notice my disappearance and that I had come with Vanessa who would be concerned as well. While hearing that made me feel worse initially, I quickly realized Jack was right - telling someone was absolutely the right thing to do. Regardless of the consequences.

My parents were definitely angry, but really it was more because of what could have happened than anything else. They were more understanding about the drinking thing than I expected, not condoning my choice and behavior, but saying that these things were somewhat expected when you were raising teenagers. I have a theory that my mom and dad tore it up when they were younger and maybe that's why they're so forgiving. But they were more concerned about what Todd did and how I was coping. Anyway, despite being somewhat cool, I was grounded for some time. Plus, I quickly realized that thinking I could keep it all hush-hush was laughable. How could I have forgotten, even momentarily, that we live in a small town where everyone knows everyone else's business and that gossip would fly – if not from seeing and hearing Blake and I argue on the pool deck, to his rapid exit and him carrying me to his truck, to the way Todd looked at school – folks were sure to be asking questions or making their own presumptions.

The details of what exactly went down between my parent's and Todd's is sketchy, but it wasn't long after their conversation that Todd, I heard, was shipped off to live with his aunt and uncle in Illinois. Rumor has it that his uncle works at some kind of place for troubled teenagers so I would have to imagine that's where Todd ended up. Honestly, I'm just happy to never see him again. Some people are just not good and anyone that would do what he did to someone is simply evil.

Given that situation, it seems of no real surprise I've been unsure about dating in general right now which is why I turned down every guy that asked me to be their date to prom. If I didn't tell them no directly, glares from Jack when anyone dared approach me kept a few at bay and I was grateful. He had become a bit overprotective since Todd - and normally I would be angry at his interference, but I've been thankful instead.

Which is how I ended up with the hottest date.

Vanessa.

Standing in my bedroom in a red silk gown that hugs her curves, she looks beautiful. We had a great time getting ready. We got our nails and hair done, did our makeup together and then slipped our dresses on and couldn't stop smiling at each other.

Tonight will be fun; going with my best friend means no pressure. No putting on a show. No worrying about saying or doing the wrong thing in front of some guy that I don't really care about impressing, but feel like I should anyway because of the money he spent on the night.

Besides they always say that prom is supposed to be a night you'll never forget in our high school lives. If that's the case then I'm guaranteed a good time with my best friend as my "date."

"Sienna!" my mom calls and knocks on my bedroom door, "Are you two ready? I'd like to take some photos before you leave."

"We'll be right out," I call to her grabbing the pink glittery lipgloss I have on my lips and placing it inside my evening clutch.

"Ready?" I ask Vanessa smiling at her admiring herself in the mirror.

"Yes. You?"

"Yep. You look really great," I tell her for the tenth time.

"So do you. That color goes with your skin tone perfectly. Blake is going to d-i-e when he sees you."

Shaking my head I roll my eyes, "I don't care about that."

Lies. My skin prickles when I think about Blake seeing me in this dress. Will he think I look pretty? Do a double take when he sees me? Wish I were his date instead of freaking Hailey? I wish I didn't care either way, but I can't help but imagine it anyway.

Looking at myself one more time, I admire the champagne colored sequin dress that hugs my body until it flares out at my mid-thigh and falls to the floor. The spaghetti straps look delicate against my skin and I turn yet again and see how they cross in the back exposing most of my back. When I move, a slit up to mid-thigh makes my leg play peek-a-boo when I walk. My gold heels with straps across the top of my foot give me a little more height and my pretty but simple diamond earrings and bracelet are the perfect accessories. I had my hair done in long waves and the sides are braided and pulled back. My eye makeup is dramatic with a simple lip and looking at myself in the mirror, I'm astonished at how it all came together.

"Okay, well I know better and he's going to forget Hailey's name when he sees you."

Ignoring her I point to the door, "Let's go before my mom starts beating down the door. I'm sure she'll take a lot of photos, so prepare yourself."

Laughing we link arms and walk out the door and into the living room. Jack is already there sporting his tux and I admit he looks very handsome. His date is a nice girl, a cheerleader named Amelia, and they've been on a few dates. They're double dating with Blake and Hailey, of course.

One night they were making plans and Vanessa and I walked into the kitchen to grab a snack. Jack said something about getting a limo and Vanessa squealed and told them all the reasons why they should definitely do that. Jack insisted we go with them. I declined not wanting to be in the same group as Blake and Hailey - I didn't really need a front and center seat next to them. Vanessa's excitement at rolling up in a limo made me keep my feelings to myself. Knowing how I was feeling regarding going with a guy, Vanessa, being the most excellent friend that she is, turned down every guy that asked her as well and said we would be each other's date this year. Given the sacrifice she made for me, the least I could do is be uncomfortable during a ride to school since she's excited.

Mom was already snapping all kinds of pictures of Jack and he was striking a different pose for each one. She had no idea he was doing it in a mocking way, she was simply delighted. Dad however was standing behind mom with a small smile on his face and his arms crossed watching Jack's antics.

My dad hears us enter and turns, "Wow, you girls look beautiful," he smiles broadly.

Mom turns to us and to my horror she gets all glassy-eyed. "Oh girls, look at you. You look so wonderful, beautiful. Time for pictures!" She sniffles and I look at Vanessa with wide eyes.

Turning I see Jack staring at us too, the look on his face almost comical. You'd think he's never seen me before, his eyebrows inch up his face in surprise and he looks from me and Vanessa and back again. He whistles low. "Wow. You clean up nice, sis."

"Shut up," I reply, but smile.

We pose for photos and laugh when we take one striking a traditional prom pose with Vanessa standing behind me with her arms wrapped around me. Giggling, we have fun with it and then when Amelia arrives we move out of the way so mom can get some pictures of the two of them.

"Let's go out on the porch," mom suggests. "The sun is just starting to go down and it will be beautiful lighting for a group photo."

"Cool, Blake should be here any minute too," Jack responds before offering his arm to Amelia with a flourish. She giggles and they head outside.

With shakes of our heads we head to the door too and I begin to feel nervous about seeing Blake and Hailey together. "Oh, I forgot my clutch, I'll be right there, go ahead," I tell Vanessa and go back into my room to grab my gold bag. I check it once more to make sure everything's inside and then take one more look at myself. My trembling hands smooth my dress down and I take a deep breath before I push my shoulders back and go to meet everyone outside.

When I reach the front door, I see Blake through the security screen and stop. The screen is dark and I can see out but he can't see inside. I'm grateful because it allows me a moment to collect myself after getting a glimpse of him.

I spent a stupid amount of time imagining what Blake would look like in a tux. I didn't come close. My imagination didn't do him justice. At all.

He's standing with his hands in his pockets, his hair slicked back off his face but stubborn waves still tumble over his forehead. If I close my eyes I can imagine how he smells - like spice and summer. He reminds me of days spent outside in the grass with the sun shining on my face and happiness in my heart. He speaks with my dad and I'm only able to capture his profile. Given my thoughts and feelings from this viewpoint, I quickly wonder what I'll feel when facing him straight-on. I'm not sure I'll survive it.

A car pulls up and I watch as Hailey arrives. She, of course, looks great. Her dress is short. A black number that dips dangerously in the front and I'm thinking she shouldn't bend over. Or maybe move much - at all. Blake takes her hand and begins walking up to our porch.

Taking a deep breath, I open the front door and step out looking first at Vanessa before my eyes automatically turn to, and connect with, Blake's. The moment they do, it feels like time stands still.

He stops walking suddenly and his lips part in surprise. His gaze sweeps over me in a way that makes a flush run over my skin in a wave starting with the tips of my toes and moving to the top of my head. When his eyes meet mine again, all the air leaves my lungs because I could swear the look on his face, in his eyes, could only be described as *need*.

My chest begins rising and falling sharply, air feeling impossible to obtain. I was right; getting a complete look of how Blake looks tonight is simply show-stopping. He looks magnificent. From the cut of his tux, the sharp envy invoking cheekbones, his dark hair and bright green-eyes, everything else disappears and all I see is him.

As if in a trance, he starts moving toward me again and I seem to come back to myself as Vanessa moves up beside me.

"You okay?" She whispers to me and I manage a nod.

Hailey's gaze narrows as she looks from Blake to me and back again.

"Let's get a photo of the whole group together before you leave," my mom says.

As if her speaking breaks a spell, Blake breaks his stare and helps Hailey manage the steps of the porch in her heels. Moving to where my mom indicates, my stomach dips when Blake comes and stands next to me. My breath catches when his arm brushes my own before he wraps his arm around my waist. I tell myself it isn't a big deal since his other is wrapped around Hailey. It's just for the photo, but my skin underneath his touch feels like it's on fire.

In-between photos he bends down and whispers in my ear, "Wow, Si. You look so beautiful."

My eyes immediately snap to his and the fire I see staring back at me almost makes my heart stop. Somehow I manage to reply, "Thanks. You look pretty good yourself."

"Thank you everyone for being so great with the photos - can I trouble you for one more? I need one with Jack, Blake and Sienna, of course."

Jack positions me in the middle with him and Blake on either side of me. Before she snaps the photo, Jack says,

"Yeah, we look *good*," making me look up at Blake and laugh while he looks down at me and shakes his head with a grin.

During the photo the limo pulls up and Vanessa claps her hands with excitement.

"Let's go!" Jack calls and moves to Amelia helping her down the stairs. "See ya, mom and dad. Don't wait up!"

They laugh at Jack and my dad pulls me to the side, "Have fun, tonight. Be careful," he tells me. I know he's still concerned after everything that happened with Todd. I give him a kiss on the cheek, "Don't worry about me."

Vanessa is already at the limo door and she giddily looks back at me over her shoulder as the limo driver holds the door open for her and helps her inside. She's embarrassingly excited about a stupid limo ride and I can't help but giggle a little.

"Let me help you," Blake captures my attention with his words and I turn to see him holding his hand out for me waiting to be my anchor as I move down the stairs. I place my hand in his and he grips mine tightly as I make my way down.

"Thank you," I murmur and it's then I realize that he helped me before Hailey and I hear her clear her throat in what sounds like annoyance.

Getting into the limo, I can't help but grin at Vanessa who's bouncing up and down in her seat with excitement. Blake slides in and sits next to me and suddenly my senses are overwhelmed with the unique scent that's him and my stomach dips and my mouth waters. He smells amazing. I look at Vanessa and give her a wide-eyed look which I hope signals my desire for help, but she just grins at me and wags her eyebrows.

We make light conversation all the way to the hotel where our event is being hosted. More than once I catch

Blake staring at my leg that's completely on display due to the slit in my dress and my crossed legs. My entire body is aware of every single move he makes the whole ride and it's a relief when we finally reach our destination.

Vanessa and I link arms again with a smile before we head into the hotel and make our way to the ballroom. At the entryway, I stop and we both take it all in. When I had heard the theme was going to be Starry Night I rolled my eyes at the stupid prom cliché, but wow, I was wrong to make fun. They went all out. There are twinkling lights everywhere, wrapped around columns, draped with tulle from place to place. Somehow they even managed to make a starry sky above our heads. But the real show-stopper is the huge crescent moon hanging from the ceiling. It's amazing.

We don't get long to gawk before our friends surround us and everyone ooh's and aah's at each other's looks. We give abundant compliments and graciously accept our own. Suddenly a good song starts playing and we all giggle and immediately proceed to the dance floor once we set our bags at a table claiming it. The dance floor is already full and people having fun, laughing, and dancing together while they sing the words to the song. I let the music wash over me and take me away. There's something about the atmosphere, my best friend laughing beside me and a great song that makes a wide smile spread across my face and I lose myself in the moment.

I've been here all of fifteen minutes or so and I'm already so glad I came. I would not have wanted to miss this. Vanessa and I grin again when another song plays, then another. It isn't long before we're gasping for breath.

"Drinks?" Vanessa asks and I nod.

We make a beeline for the refreshment table. Filling our

glasses we take them to our table and sit down to cool off and enjoy our drinks.

"Look at Amber's dress, I love it," I tell Vanessa. Our friend looks like a mermaid in the sparkly blue dress that hugs her figure before flaring out at the bottom. "She's one of the only people I know that can pull off that look."

"For sure," Vanessa agrees.

"Oh my god. Did you see Rosalyn?" I ask about one of Hailey's best friends. My nose wrinkles as I take in her appearance again.

"Can you say ho?" Vanessa asks with a disgusted look. "Could it be any shorter?"

"How are her boobs staying in that thing? It's cut so low."

"They've got to be all taped to hell," Vanessa adds.

"How did she even get in the door?" I marvel.

"Probably because pervy Pearson was at the door," Vanessa states, referencing the teacher everyone is convinced spends more time leering at the girls at school than he does teaching them.

We're in the middle of a lively debate about who will be named Junior Prom Queen and King when we're interrupted.

"Sienna?"

Looking up my gaze connects with West. He's a senior and incredibly good looking. He plays for our school's hockey team and I don't know if he's ever spoken to me a day in my life.

"Yes?"

He smiles and I'm instantly transfixed by his cute boyish charm. His smile is almost shy. "I was wondering if you want to dance? With me?"

"Me?" I ask in confusion. "What about your date?" I ask knowing he's got to be here with someone. I don't think he's dating anyone that I know of, but still last thing I need is to piss someone off.

"Cece and I came as friends. She's dancing with Ryan right now," he points over his shoulder.

I look at Vanessa and she smiles and nods. "Okay," I agree and West holds his hand out to me. I put my hand in his and he pulls me onto the dance floor. He wraps his hands around my waist and I place mine at his shoulders. We begin to move to the song. Nerves make my stomach turn.

"You look very pretty tonight," he compliments.

"Thanks, you too," then I flush, "I mean, you look nice too."

"Thanks," he grins. "You know, I caught some of your volleyball games this year."

"You did?" But of course I already knew that. All the girls were aflutter when he attended. I was too involved in winning to give a crap.

"You're really good."

"Thank you."

"I'm playing hockey in college. Got a scholarship actually," he brags.

"That's great."

"You should come to one of my hockey games this year," he invites. He's attending Montana State - the whole school was talking about when he accepted, surprised he didn't choose to leave the state instead.

Smiling I nod, "Maybe I will."

"Awesome."

He turns me and I look around at the couples around us as West tells me about the teams he's excited to play against. I see Jack dancing with Amelia and when he bends down to kiss her I look away.

Next my gaze connects with Blake's. He's dancing with Hailey. She's got her face shoved against his chest, eyes closed, body pressed against his tightly. She's totally into it clearly, but I don't know if I can say the same about him since he's clearly zoned in on me. I quickly look away.

West's hand moves down my arm and I can't help but look Blake's direction again and watch as his eyes track the movement before he looks back into my eyes. His lips are pressed in a firm line and if I didn't know better I'd say he appears... jealous. That can't be it though. I'm sure he's just being overprotective after everything that happened earlier this year. I doubt he wants to clean up another Sienna mess.

I smile at him reassuringly, and he smiles back, but it looks forced.

"Don't you think?" West asks and I have no idea what he was talking about.

"Um, sure."

"Yeah, me too," he says and I smile.

When the song ends I step away, "Thank you for the dance." A fast song begins playing and he looks a bit annoyed. "I should go back to Vanessa," I tell him pointing over my shoulder. As if on cue, Cece comes to his side to get his attention which facilitates my escape.

Vanessa is still where I left her, "West Jenkins asked you to dance!"

I smile, "It was... nice."

"Nice? Just nice? I'm pretty sure there's a bunch of girls that would die to dance with him and you just called it *nice*?"

I shrug. "Should we go take our prom photos?"

"I thought you'd never ask!"

We head to wait in line for the photo booth set up and discuss how we should pose, resulting in standing back to back giving sultry looks to the camera, before grabbing a bunch of props and laughing at ourselves the whole time. I have no idea how they are going to turn out, but I can't wait to see them.

When another good song begins to play, we look at each other, smile and quickly head to the dance floor again. They play a favorite fast song, and then another and we once again break out all our best moves, laughing at each other as we try to one up each other. My feet start to hurt a bit and I point at them and gesture to the chairs. Vanessa nods her head, gives me a thumbs up and a huge smile, and keeps dancing.

Getting a fresh drink, I head to an empty table to rest my feet for a bit. I'm not alone long before West approaches me again but this time he's got a few of his friends, Brian, Jeremy, and Mario with him. They all sit down with me.

"Look at Keith," West points out to the dance floor and we all laugh when we see Keith, a regular class clown doing what he probably thinks is some cool break dance moves, but unfortunately, he just manages to look ridiculous.

"My brother doesn't look much better," I tease and everyone laughs when they see Jack really feeling himself on the dance floor. His moves are over the top and he's gaining a lot of attention as people surround him laughing.

Looking away, once again my eyes collide with Blake's. He's on the dance floor, surrounded by people, but he's standing still. He's looking at my table and he keeps looking from person to person. The smile falls off my face surprised by how irritated he looks. Confused, I look away and paste a smile on my face as I listen to the guys talk about other people's dance moves.

"Mine are better than all of theirs," Mario says.

"Sure, they are," I tease.

He looks at me, mirth in his eyes and he gets out of his seat to show me said moves. We're all laughing at his thrusting and grinding when suddenly the music changes and he immediately starts looking around in confusion, which makes us all laugh again.

West looks at me and stands. I know he's about to ask me to dance again. Should I? I still can't help but feel like it's not right considering he has a date here. He really should be dancing with her. Then again, I guess she's not complaining.

"Want to dance with me?" Mario asks surprising me.

"Me?" I ask surprised.

West looks immediately annoyed and says, "Dude!"

Mario shrugs.

"No. She's going to dance with me."

My insides fall at the sound of his voice. I didn't see or hear Blake approach too caught up in those around me. My head snaps in his direction. "What?" I ask in shock.

"Will you please dance with me, Si?"

As it always does when he's near, everything else becomes inconsequential and I find myself nodding and he's smiling as he pulls me onto the dance floor, but not before I capture him giving what appears to be a mocking smile to the guys at the table.

His arms wrap around my waist and he pulls me close. My heart stutters and for a moment I'm afraid I'm going to make a fool of myself and collapse - dramatic I know - but he makes me feel irrational at times.

"Won't Hailey be mad?" I ask.

He shrugs, "You and I have been best friends forever. No way I wasn't going to have at least one dance with you tonight. She can have a problem with it all she wants," he says matter-of-fact.

Sometimes I hate that word. *Friends.* Yay, me.

Choosing to take advantage of the moment, I place my ear against his chest as we sway side-to-side and I could be mistaking, but I'm pretty sure his heart is pounding as fast as mine.

"Are you having fun?"

I can feel his chest rumble with his words and it makes my cheek tingle. "I am," I admit. "I wasn't sure I would, but I really am."

"Good," he murmurs. "That's good."

"Are you?" I ask in return.

He shrugs.

"So, when are you and Jack going to finally tell me where you're going to college?" I ask. The two of them made a decision a few weeks ago, but have been quiet about their decision - not telling me a thing. No one knows where they're going except our parents, and Blake's family I'm guessing, but no one is surprised that whatever they've decided it's clear they're going together. There's been a lot of hushed conversations at home, sometimes a feeling of tension which I find confusing, and it's starting to drive me a little crazy.

"I actually want to talk to you about that. Can you spare some time for me this week? So we can talk?"

Is the sky blue? Are unicorns majestic? Does a unibrow need waxed? What does he think?

"Yeah, of course," I nod keeping my cool.

"Good," he says softly, tugging me closer as another slow song begins playing as soon as the last one ends.

"Can I cut in?" West asks.

"No," Blake says sharply. Surprised at his tone, I remove my cheek from his chest to look up at him and find him glaring behind me to where West is clearly standing. "We're talking."

"That wasn't very nice," I tell him.

He shrugs at me, a small smile pulls up his mouth in the corner, a dimple winking at me.

"West is a tool. Cares about the hockey stick in his pants maybe as much as the one in his hands during a game if you get my drift."

"He seems nice," I reply

He makes a noise of disagreement.

"When I'm not here next year, promise me you'll be careful. Smart."

Here he goes again with the big brother stuff. Just once I'd like to pretend that isn't all he feels for me. That he saw me tonight and regretted his date choice of Hailey instead of me. That after seeing me, he realized he has feelings for me, that he wants to be with me. I almost laugh out loud. All the fantasies of a stupid girl.

"I promise, Blake. The thing that happened with Todd, I'm moving past that; I *have* to get past that. You and Jack have to let me or I'll live in fear and seclusion all the time. And that would not be the way I'd prefer to spend my senior year."

"I get that, but you still need to be cautious."

"I will. I'll be fine."

Pulling away from him, heart aching at the big brother bit, I smile up at him, but it feels forced. "Thank you for the dance," I tell him before spinning around and walking away. I can't help it, I turn to glimpse at him over my shoulder and find him watching me walk away with a conflicted look on his face.

I make a beeline for the refreshment table, needing a drink again to cool off again. A teacher that's chaperoning smiles at me and pours my drink. I thank her and take a few steps to the side, knowing I may need a refill soon and stay close.

"You're only managing to look pathetic, you know."

Jumping a little in surprise at the person suddenly next to me, I feel a look of annoyance cross my face. "What are you talking about, Hailey?"

"Everyone knows you're hard up for Blake. When you look at him, you look at him the way a fat virgin looks at the last dude in a bar on her twenty-first birthday."

"What the hell does that even mean?"

"It means that you can keep wishing all you want, but Blake is never going to look at you as anything other than a little sister."

"I'm *not* his sister."

"You may as well be. You're nothing more to him. No matter what you wish were true."

"If that's the only way he looks at me, why are you so worried and warning me off of him?" I ask bravely. I know she's right, but I'll be damned if I'll let her harass me or tell me what to do. Not anymore.

Her nostrils flare and her eyes narrow, "Stay away from him," she says before purposefully bumping her shoulder into mine and spilling her drink down the front of my dress.

I gasp and squeal, shaking my arms at my side to try and get some of the liquid off of me.

"You bitch!" I say looking at Hailey's smug and stupid face.

"Don't you forget it," she sneers.

Vanessa appears out of nowhere with napkins, "Oh my gosh, come on," she says and drags me out of the ballroom.

"I hate her," I tell Vanessa, tears coming to my eyes.

"I know. She's just jealous. It's okay. We'll take care of this."

She escorts me into the bathroom and I stand there while Vanessa takes care of my dress. I watch silently, trying to hold the tears at bay the whole time.

"Did you see the way Blake is looking at you tonight? How his attention has been on you constantly, following you around the room?"

"No," I whisper.

She stops and makes eye contact with me, "Well, it has been."

"So what? He sees me in a pretty dress and all the sudden it's like oh wow, she has boobs. She's a girl. I should pay attention to her? Whatever."

"I don't think that's what's going on," Vanessa says. "There. All better."

I look down and though it still feels damp, there's no red at all. She saved my dress, but I have no idea how.

"Thank you," I tell her, lip quivering before I bite it to gain control.

"Don't let her make you upset. She's a ho bag."

I laugh, "I know." I sniff and lift my chin.

"Okay?"

"Okay."

She nods and we leave the bathroom together, but I stop short when I see Blake standing down the hall arguing with Hailey. I can't hear everything they're saying but he looks angry. His head turns to mine and he says something to her again before walking away from her. She glares at me, hate burning in her gaze, before she walks away.

Blake looks at Vanessa and nods, before looking at me, "Are you okay?"

"I'm fine."

"I saw what she did. I'm sorry."

Anger suddenly washes over me in a burning wave. I

feel my cheeks flush and my fists clench, "Why are you even with her? For the life of me, I can't understand it. I'm sorry, I tried," I lie. I never tried, but whatever, that's irrelevant. "I just don't get it."

"Well, clearly that's been a mistake."

"Wh-what?"

"I'm done with her. What she did isn't okay. Can I give you a ride home?"

"How? We came here in a limo."

He holds up car keys, "I borrowed a car," he looks at Vanessa. "I can give you a ride too, if you'd like?"

She looks at me, then Blake, and back again. "If it's okay with you, I'd like to stay. I'll get a ride home from someone or call my mom. A few people asked if you and I wanted to go grab a bite to eat after anyway. Maybe I'll take them up on it. Unless you want to stay and go too?"

"I think I'd like to go home," I confess, my good mood ruined.

She nods, "Okay. Go, then. I'll be fine."

"Are you sure?"

She smiles, "Absolutely." She gives me a hug, kisses me on the cheek and leaves.

Blake looks at me, lifting his brows and holds out his elbow to me. I put my hand in his arm and he walks me out of the hotel. When we're outside, he clicks a button on the key fob and when a horn sounds, we begin moving in that direction.

"I borrowed Mitch's car," he says. "He said he'd catch a ride with Russell."

I remain silent and watch as he opens the door for me and waits for me to get inside before closing it and moving around the front of the car.

Once he's inside, he turns to me, "Are you hungry? Usually everyone eats after these things."

"Starving," I confess.

"Where do you want to go? Wren's Cafe? Java Jitters? The Sweet Spot?" He starts naming a bunch of places in town. "It's my treat."

Sitting down and enjoying a meal, coffee, or sweet with Blake, his attention all on me sounds nice, but really, I don't want any of those places. So instead I shake my head and say, "You know what? I'd really just like a cheeseburger," and I tell him my favorite fast food place.

He laughs, "Yeah?"

"Yep," I nod.

"Alright. One cheeseburger coming right up."

When he starts driving, I turn the radio on and search until I find a song I like. He smiles his approval when I choose one and we drive in silence, listening to the song. We go through the drive thru and order, Blake telling me he has an idea.

When we pull up to the old covered bridge that leads in and out of town, I smile. I love that bridge and I love that he knows it. There's two in town. This one, and another on private property. Kids all over town sneak onto the property and it has become a make out spot - almost like a rite of passage it seems. The story behind the bridge is rather romantic, a man named Henry Davis built it for his wife as a way for her to cross the river to the forest on their property so she could explore the forest she loved. He later proposed there and it's a meaningful monument in town now. If Blake took me there I'd probably have a heart attack. Cue the dramatics again.

"Come on," Blake looks at me with a smile.

I've barely got the door open and Blake is helping me

out of the car. I take a few steps in the direction he steers me but when my heels sink into the grass I stumble.

"Well we can't have that. Here, hold this." He gives me the bag of food along with both drinks to balance and then carefully picks me up, cradling me in his arms.

"I could have just taken my shoes off," I laugh.

He just smiles and carries me to a grassy area near the bridge and sets me down.

"Sorry I don't have a blanket or anything."

"It's fine."

"Oh wait," he takes his jacket off and spreads it on the ground.

"What if it gets grass stains or something?"

"It's fine," he shrugs.

I take a seat and immediately take my shoes off and put my toes in the grass. I catch a smile on Blake's face out of the corner of my eye when he sits next to me.

He takes the package of food and digs out my burger handing it to me.

Unwrapping it carefully, I take a huge bite and moan my happiness making Blake laugh.

"Sorry," I mumble with my mouth full. "Hungry."

He responds by taking a big bite of his own and we eat in companionable silence. The road is quiet, no one busy coming in and out of town tonight I guess.

"Mmm, hits the spot," I tell him after another bite. His eyes drop to my mouth watching me chew before he looks away and clears his throat, and runs his hand through his hair. He reaches into the bag and pulls out fries and holds them to me in silent question. I grab a few.

"How's Mandy?" I ask about his sister realizing I haven't inquired for a while at how she's doing. I don't see her around much.

"Good. Loving beauty school. I had to tell her no, that I didn't want my hair dyed bleach blonde last week." I giggle. "She's hoping to snag a job at Serenity," he says talking about the salon in town. "But she also talks about ditching this town, so I'm not sure what she'll do to be honest."

"That's cool," I nod and take another bite.

"Yeah."

"How's your mom?" I ask.

He grimaces, "Uh, let's talk about something else?"

"Yeah, of course. I'm sorry."

He nods.

"I can't believe it's almost the end of the school year," I say.

"You'll be a senior next year. Big man, or should I say woman, on campus."

"Yeah, I guess. I'm just excited for volleyball season again."

"Have you looked at any of the colleges already sending you letters?"

Shrugging, I admit, "A few."

"What looks good so far?"

"I'm not sure," I start, but something makes me stop. "Actually, that's not true. Want to know a secret?"

"Always."

"I want to leave this town."

His brows inch up his forehead, "What? Really? You do?"

"Why does that surprise you?"

"I don't know. I guess I never really asked you before. Plus with the farm and your family, I guess I just figured you'd stay close by."

"Look, if anyone takes over the farm later it will be Jack, but that's years away and who knows what might happen in the meantime. This town is just... small. There's a whole world out there. And I want to see it. Be part of it."

"I understand that."

"You do?"

"More than you know," he nods and I feel like there's more to it than he's saying, but I'm distracted by the thought when he asks me, "Where are some places you want to go?"

Smiling widely, I start naming them off on my fingers, "There's so many! Italy, New Orleans, Hawaii, Tahiti, England, California, Seattle, Boston..."

He laughs which interrupts me, "Wow, that's a hell of a list."

"I'm not finished," I laugh.

"If you could visit one tomorrow - which would you choose?"

"That's an impossible choice!" I object.

"Come on, pick one."

"Hmm, well, I've always wanted to see the ocean. Have you heard of a place called Thor's Well? It's in Oregon."

"Thor's Well? No, I haven't heard of it."

"It looks amazing. You'll have to look up a photo. It's a huge hole on the coast and it looks like it's swallowing the ocean - gallons and gallons of water falling into what looks like a bottomless sinkhole. I bet it's amazing and crazy to see in person."

"Beautiful," he says.

"Yes, I'm sure it's beautiful, it has to be," I look at him and find him staring at me and my face flushes suddenly wondering if he was talking about the place I want to visit... or me? Flustered I keep talking, "I'd love to visit places outside of the United States, but there's so much to see here too," I marvel. "You know, I've never made a list. I should make a list." He chuckles softly and I look at him again and see him smiling at me. "What?"

"I just love how animated and excited you are while talking about this."

I shrug feeling a little embarrassed, "Someday I'll see some of those places."

"I hope you do," he says quietly.

Since we're finished eating, we crumble up the wrappers and sit in silence for a bit. My mind wanders through the events of the night. With a full belly, I feel tired and relaxed. When I yawn for the third time, Blake smiles.

"Alright, let's go. Time to get Cinderella home from the ball."

"Cinderella, huh? Better hurry then before our ride turns back into a pumpkin."

He helps me stand and when my feet immediately sink into the grass again when I replace my shoes he stops me, "One second."

He takes our trash and puts it in the car to throw away later, then comes back to me and picks me up again.

"This really isn't necessary," I argue once more.

"I don't mind."

He places me in the car again and I once again find a song on the radio after he starts the car. "Can we roll down the window? It's amazing out tonight."

"Sure," he immediately finds the button and lowers them.

As we drive, the breeze moving through the car feels heavenly. It raises my hair off the back of my neck and I place one of my arms out the window and wiggle my fingers feeling the wind blow through them. My eyes close and I lose myself in the moment.

The feeling in the air is mesmerizing - when summer's

so close you can get lost in it's warmth already. Plants, trees, and flowers are all blooming making the air fragrant. Breathing in deeply, I open my eyes and look up to the sky. In the dusky sky, the stars are just starting to appear, their twinkling lights making me smile. I know when it's full night the sky will be filled with them. It won't be long before the days are much longer, the sun not setting until after nine o'clock at night, or later the deeper we get into summer. The days may feel longer but I know it will go fast and it won't be long before Blake and Jack leave me and head to wherever they've decided to go for college. Because I know them. And I know they're leaving this town just like I want to some day.

Looking over at him, I catch Blake staring at me. The way he looks at me makes me tremble. I feel like he's taking a snapshot so can revisit it later.

When we pull up to my house I can't help but feel disappointed. The time I get alone with him is... well never anymore. I feel reluctant to give it up, but it is what it is and I'll be grateful for the time we had. I know I'll store it away to dissect later. It's just the way it is – precious to me, regardless of facts and truths.

"Thank you," I tell him, turning to him, "For the ride, the burger, the company."

"You don't have to thank me for any of that."

"Well, I do all the same."

With a final smile, I pull the handle of the door and place one foot on the ground before he calls my name, "Sienna?"

"Yeah?"

I look back at him with a smile. He stares at me in that way he did earlier tonight when I walked out of my house. "I think... I think I'll always remember the way you looked tonight. You looked beautiful; no, you *are* beautiful." I swallow thickly, his words taking me off guard and making my breath catch. "I just wanted... needed... to say that."

I open my mouth but words don't come out. I don't even know how to respond. It doesn't seem to matter though because he simply smiles, "Good night."

I step out of the car and walk up to the house. My breaths come out sharply, my heart beating double time. Part of me wants to turn around and run to the car, to ask him why he said that. To demand to know what it means, if anything at all. When I open the door, I hear the car start pulling away, and I turn suddenly to run back, but stop when I see he's further away than I expected.

The moment is gone.

I stand on my porch and stare at the car long after the taillights are no longer visible.

6

I'm in one hell of a crappy mood. It started this morning when I couldn't find my favorite t-shirt which made me run late, and Jack was so irritated he grumbled at me the whole way to school. When we pulled up I saw Hailey talking to Blake and even though it didn't look like he was into the conversation it still pissed me off. Rumor is that she's willing to do "whatever it takes" to get him back. She's been around him constantly and it really annoys me. She's even gone as far as pretending to be nice to me when I'm anywhere in the vicinity of Blake and he can overhear. It's gag worthy.

My mood continued when I got my English essay back that I wrote on the book *Crime and Punishment* and I got a B+. Not an awful grade, but not the one I deserve in my opinion, but clearly my teacher doesn't agree.

They were out of my favorite soda at lunch. Henry, an annoying boy in one of my classes sneezed on me. I tripped down the hall in front of everyone and some people clapped, assholes that they are. Jessica, a girl that has a locker next to mine opened hers so hard it smacked me in the back which I'm positive left a mark.

Plus, when I should be concentrating, I remember Blake's words to me, "*I think I'll always remember the way you looked tonight.*" They run through my mind like a marathon runner and trying to define them in every which way possible is about to make me insane.

So yeah.

It was *that* kind of day.

Really, I shouldn't have been surprised when we're heading home in Jack's car after school and Blake turns to me from the front seat to tell me something that makes my stomach drop.

"Hey," he begins and I look at him in question, "Jack and I want to talk to you when we get to the house."

"Okay..."

He doesn't say anything else, just turns around and raises the volume on the radio.

I stare out the window on the ride home, feeling uneasy.

Once Jack drives down the gravel drive and parks, we all pile out of the car. Jack points off in the distance, "Come on, this is a treehouse conversation."

With my heart in my throat, I follow them to what's been our special place. Over the years, we've had what we've dubbed some very serious conversations. They've ranged from debates over what video game is best and why, who the best football player really is in school, and which is better *Marvel* or *DC*. A particularly lively one was whether or not ice cream should be eaten with cake or not. My vote was no, makes cake soggy which is totally gross.

More serious conversations included things like Jack confessing his first crush, even his most recent - Amelia. It's where I confessed that I stole a lipgloss from a local store in town because mom wouldn't buy it for me and I was angry. The most serious thing though was when Blake once told us how much he misses his dad. He left the family and no one has heard from him since. Blake confessed he often wonders where he is, what he's doing, and if he ever thinks about them.

It's always been "our" place and I know if they're taking me there to talk it's because it's important. Not something as simple as "Let's celebrate because we're going to Montana U."

When Blake told me at prom that he'd like time to talk to me this week, I assumed it was just going to be the two of us. Clearly, as I trail the two of them I realize that's not the case, and I can't help but feel frustrated. This is clearly something they planned, and it definitely makes sense that Jack wants to be part of what they're telling me since clearly it's something they're doing together, but I selfishly want alone time with Blake - since prom it's all I can think about.

Various scenarios have run through my mind ranging from one extreme to another. I imagined finally being alone with him and demanding to know why he said what he did to me about looking and being beautiful. I want to ask him why he seemed jealous and possessive at the dance. I even had fantasies about simply walking up to him and putting my mouth on his. Thoughts that make my breaths come fast and heat wash over me in streams. It made me wonder what it would be like to kissed by Blake. Would he grasp my chin with his slender flingers and kiss me soft and slow? Or would he press his body against mine, grasp my hair in a handful and kiss me with fiery passion and heat?

I almost laugh out loud thinking about it now because there's no chance in hell of any of that happening. Since the dance, Blake has been back to business as usual. It's like that night was just a dream.

"Alright, what's the big deal? Why the treehouse?" I ask looking at them both in confusion, but also a touch of mirth hints in the curve of my lips at the dramatic nature of this.

"No questions," Jack says as we reach the large sycamore on our property and jerks his thumb at the ladder. "Just climb."

Rolling my eyes, I sigh but I saunter past them both and climb up, eager to get this underway and find out the big news.

Once I'm up, I take a seat on the floor leaning my back against the wall and cross my legs at the ankle waiting for them to get settled. They sit as well, across from me, then look back and forth between each other.

Raising my brows, I finally ask, "What is the big deal? You guys are acting weird. Just spit it out, I already know you're leaving Mason Creek to go to college. It's obvious. Just tell me where you're going already and why it's been such a secret."

"That's not exactly true," Jack hedges.

"What? That you're going out of town or that you're acting weird?" Blake watches me carefully while I look between the two of them.

"It's not true that we're leaving town for college."

"Really?" I ask and that one word is full of hope and happiness. I can't stop a smile from spreading across my mouth, but it drops when I see they aren't smiling too.

"Look, Sienna, the truth is-"

Blake cuts Jack off, "We asked your parents if we could tell you. Alone. They weren't sure, at first but we told them it's how you'd want it to be."

"Okay..."

Jack scratches his brow, "We told them we wanted to wait until everything was all worked out before we told you our decision."

"It isn't going to be easy for us to leave you," Blake says and he runs his hands through his hair like he always does when he's frustrated or nervous. The gesture raises my unease a notch and emotion clogs my throat.

"We'll miss each other, I know," I reply. "It will be really weird. I mean, it's been the three of us... for so long. I can't imagine being left here-" Suddenly my throat clogs up and it cuts off my words making me feel embarrassed. I clear my throat and blink several times trying to push back the burn behind my eyes.

They look at each other with alarm. If I had it in me, I'd laugh. What is it with the male species?

"Look guys, will you stop? I'll be fine. I have Vanessa, remember? Yeah, the three of us used to call ourselves the three musketeers - really original by the way - but the truth is, it's been a long time since it's been that way. As we grew up and our interests changed, we kind of went our separate ways with some things. I haven't hung out with you constantly or followed you around since we were kids you know," I smile with fondness.

"We know, but that doesn't matter. We've always been *here*. Had your back when you did, and probably when you didn't, know it. You mean everything to us," Blake says hoarsely and the emotion churning in his eyes takes me off guard.

"No matter what we'll always be there for you," Jack adds. "Just like we always have been."

"You guys are seriously making this into a melodrama like that one movie channel mom watches."

"Sienna-" Blake begins but then Jack blurts, "We

enlisted in the Army," before Blake finishes whatever he was going to say.

They both freeze.

I freeze.

It's like they've just dropped a bomb and they're waiting for it to explode.

I laugh nervously, "That's funny, guys. Now tell me the truth."

They look at each other and then back at me. Blake shakes his head a little and I look back and forth between the two of them not finding a speck of humor in their gazes. Blake runs his hand through his hair again. Jack slides his hands down his thighs over and over like his palms are damp and he's trying to dry them.

"You're serious?"

Solemnly, they both nod.

A flush runs up my body so quickly, I feel dizzy. Sweat breaks out on my forehead and I suddenly feel like I can't breathe.

I stand up suddenly.

Startled the guys both stand too.

They exchange looks but keep their distance.

I begin pacing the small space my thoughts whirling through my mind so fast I can't grasp onto one to give it voice.

I feel like I may be sick.

I sit back down again.

The guys look at each other and immediately sit too.

"Why?" I finally ask. "What about football?"

"Football is great, we love it," Jack starts.

"But it isn't a realistic future. As great as we want to believe we are, we aren't going to go pro or anything," Blake finishes.

"Still, why?"

"My dad was military," Blake says as if this explains everything.

"I want to make a difference," Jack says and I want to laugh, but I can't.

"There are a lot of ways to make a difference that don't involve potentially losing your life," I say.

"Sienna, we could die in a car crash tomorrow," Jack tries to reason, but my glare shuts him up.

"How long?" I ask, and I'm vaguely surprised that my voice sounds hoarse.

"Our initial commitment is four years," Jack says.

"But we'll start with boot camp," Blake says softly.

"We'll get to come home for a little bit after that," Jack adds.

"And then?" I ask.

"And then we'll have more training," Blake says.

"We'll come home as often as we can," Jack says quickly as if that makes this all better, but I know that he's just trying to make me feel better because I know damn well breaks aren't as frequent as he's trying to make it sound.

"And after training?"

They look at each other, "Eventually we'll be stationed somewhere," Blake says softly.

I stand again feeling like I need to move.

The guys stand too.

Any other time I may laugh at this up and down dance we're doing.

"How long?" I ask again.

"Four years active duty. Two years inactive," Blake says softly as if speaking louder will startle me.

"We won't even likely stay together either," Jack adds.

"How long?" I ask again, gritting my teeth.

"Plus we could be deployed fast, I mean we really have no idea when or if that could happen. There's no way to know," Jack shrugs as if it's no big deal.

But it is.

It's a very big deal.

They have no idea the storm that's brewing before them. They don't understand what I'm asking. I vacillate between wanting to strangle them and demanding to know what they're thinking. I want to hug them and beg them not to go. I want to cry and tell them I'm proud of their choice. I want to push them out of the treehouse and hurt them badly enough that they can't go anywhere. Ever.

I laugh.

It bubbles up from somewhere deep and it bursts out of me before I can stifle it down.

I know it sounds crazy, but I can't help it.

Jack takes a step toward me, concern furrowing his brow, "Sienna?"

"Don't," I hold a hand up stopping him in his tracks.

I move to the corner and face away from them trying to gain control of myself. I feel a sob rise in my throat and I hear a shoe scuff the floor. Whirling around, both of them freeze in place.

"How. long. until. you. leave." I grit out. Which is what I've been asking all along.

I don't need or want to know the specifics about when they're in boot camp versus training versus when they'll get stationed where and how. I'm not stupid. I already know the free time that they'll have in-between all these things will be minimal. I know that they'll basically live their life at the mercy of the military telling them where to go and when to be there.

I don't need the details to know that everything is changing.

Everything has already changed.

They look at each other again and I know, I just know what they're going to say. Because graduation is next month and I know, I *know* they're leaving afterward.

"We leave the day after graduation," Blake says quietly, another bomb dropped in our small space.

I knew it. I nod. And I nod again.

"We signed up a couple months ago, so we have to report in a month."

"Sienna, talk to us," Blake pleads.

"What do you want me to say?" I ask spreading my arms out wide.

Jack takes a step toward me again but stops when I glare. He sighs and sounds desperate when he asks, "Tell us what you're thinking."

"I'm thinking..." I stop and look away, needing to take a deep breath before I continue. "I'm thinking that I'm angry that you're just now telling me."

They open their mouths, "Yes, but-"

"Do you want to know what I'm feeling and thinking or not?" I snap.

Their brows both raise in unison at my tone and they smartly keep quiet.

"I don't know why or how you could possibly have thought that one month would have been enough time for me to come to terms with this. It's not like it's something you've talked about over the years. It feels like it came out of left field." I pause again because I don't want emotions to overwhelm me and make me unable to say what I want to say.

"I'm hurt because you didn't involve me in your decision,

not because I would change your mind, but because this is *huge*. And I feel stupid because I'm hurt that for the first time you didn't include me in a decision about something that's so big... so monumental."

Pausing, I take a deep breath.

"Sienna," Blake tries to interject.

"No. I'm not done." He nods and Jack's teeth clench so hard I can see the muscles protrude in his jaw.

"I guess I need to get used to that anyway, right? Not being included in things," I laugh without humor. "I'm also thinking that I'm going to miss you *so much* it physically hurts. It feels like I can't breathe," and the tears fall now. I'm helpless to stop them.

Blake and Jack both continue to look pained.

Blake runs his hand through his hair - again - and this time I almost lose it completely. It's such a simple gesture, and one I'm going to miss seeing with all my heart.

"I'm wondering why this? Why is this the direction you decided to take?"

"Because-"

I don't even know who spoke, I ignore them. "I'm scared. I'm so scared something will happen to you both, but I'm also so fucking proud of you too." Their eyes widen at my language knowing I don't use it often. "A choice like this can't have come easy and I'm thinking that you've both always been my own personal heroes, now I'm just going to have to share you with the whole United States too."

They can't contain themselves anymore, they come to me and both wrap their arms around me. I try, I really try to hold it in, but I can't.

I let go.

Big, deep, heartfelt sobs leave me. My legs give out and they ease me to the floor.

Yes, it's been different these past years as we grew up and naturally grew apart in some ways, but that's totally different than them not being here at all. At least with college we would have had Spring, Fall, Winter, and Summer break. Not going to happen now with the Army.

They each take turns holding on to me and letting me cry. They whisper words of compassion and comfort while rocking me back and forth.

I don't know how much time passes, but eventually I pull away.

Wet spots are on each of their shirts and I should probably feel embarrassed, but I don't.

"I came prepared," Jack says and pulls a bundle of Kleenex from his pocket.

"You're just now giving these to me?" I ask and yank them from his hands to sop up the wetness under my eyes and nose.

"Sorry, I forgot."

"Sienna," Blake says hesitantly, "We waited to tell you what we were considering and then what we decided until the school year was almost over because we didn't want it to affect your year. We knew it would be hard, for all of us, and harder once you knew and we just wanted to enjoy the rest of the year with you without this hanging over our heads."

"And as far as why, well there's lots of reasons," Jack says. "The state of the world makes us angry and instead of complaining about it, we want to *do* something about it."

What if they die? I try to shut down the thought immediately, but I can't help it. I'm sure it has to be a worry anyone would have in this position. It's impossible to not worry about their safety; their lives.

"If you both don't mind, I'd like some time alone."

"But-" Blake begins to protest.

"I need you to do this for me," I say sternly standing.

They nod and stand as well. Jack steps to me and hugs me before heading down the ladder. Blake stares at me and I wish I knew what he was thinking. He reaches out a hand, my breath catches when he pushes my hair out of my face and behind my ear. "You're one of my best friends."

"I know," I tell him.

"I love you," he says simply, and I stop breathing. "I have since we were kids, and I always will. You're my family," he tells me and it takes all I have to remain composed.

"Yeah, I know, Blake. I love you too," I whisper knowing that those words have a different meaning to me than they do to him. My love for him isn't in the way a sister loves a brother. It's more.

He stares at me for a moment before following Jack and heading down the ladder.

I move to the treehouse window and watch them walk away. A sob catches in my throat again and I cover my mouth with my hand.

This feels surreal. Like a nightmare I'll wake up from and somehow laugh at the insanity my mind conjured. But no, it's real. It's real and it feels tragic.

Once, when I was reading Romeo and Juliet we had a discussion in class about it of course, but it prompted me to look up the definition of tragedy. It's a word used so often about the story and it prompted my curiosity.

Tragedy, a noun, defining an event that causes great suffering, destruction, and distress. Doesn't that perfectly encapsulate the state my relationship with Blake? I think so.

We're simply tragic.

A perfect tragedy.

7

*W*hen it's time to start getting ready for Blake and Jack's graduation and going away party, the first thing I do is take a long and luxurious bath. I'm not one for baths, usually because I'm always in a hurry, but today, I stay under the water until my skin is wrinkly. I spend the day being lazy, trying to forget my sadness by getting lost in my favorite author's book, but even the world she created can't help me forget my own.

While I get ready, I use the time to try to relax my emotions, my mind, and to brace myself for today and the tough ones that will follow.

I want to look good today. I'd be lying if I didn't admit it occurs to me that how I look today will be one of the last memories Blake has of me. I slather my body in sweet smelling lotion, curl my hair, and select a white and blue floral dress that makes me feel pretty. I'm applying the finishing touches to my makeup when I hear my mom and the friends she's recruited to help set up for the party begin working in the kitchen. Their laughter gets louder and louder and I have no doubt alcohol is at least partially responsible.

I'm thankful for the light heartedness and laughs they offer; it sounds like she's enjoying herself.

Mom has been emotional about Jack leaving. She tries to hide it, but it's still evident. In part, she's been trying to show support for his decision. But I also think she worries outward displays of her sadness would make me feel worse, her grief adding to mine. I anticipate that we will be able to bring comfort to each other later.

Today isn't that day though.

Not wanting to be roped into helping or answering questions like, "Are you sad your brother is leaving?" or "How do you feel about Jack joining the Army?" I sneak out the back door of the house when I'm ready and make my way to the barn.

It's a beautiful day out. There's a soft breeze in the air and it makes the stalks of wheat in our field do a swaying dance that sounds and smells like home. I think as long as I live I'll love that soft rustling sound. Sometimes I like to leave my bedroom window open at night so I can hear the wind sift through the wheat - it soothes me to sleep. The sun lowering in the sky turns the field golden in color and it's a sight any photographer would swoon over.

In the background, a horse neighs, making me smile, and it directs my attention back to the barn and I hasten my steps. Spending time with our many animals always helps relax me and brings me joy. When I enter, one of our horses, Cupcake, announces her greeting immediately making it known she requires my attention.

"Hi, sweet girl," I speak lovingly as I rub her long nose and reach into the nearby bag of sugar cubes to give her a treat. "Today is going to be a tough day. Have you ever heard the phrase 'fake it til you make it'?"

Her head bobs and I laugh out loud - I love the timing.

"That's gonna be me. Faking it, pretending that I'm not dying a little inside at the thought of Jack and Blake leaving. I'm trying to stop feeling so selfish about this, because I am proud of them, glad they're doing what they feel they should, but it's hard. Does that make me a bad person?"

Her big brown eyes with full lashes look into mine and I can almost imagine compassion for how I'm feeling. I kiss her nose.

"I promise I'll come back and take you for a ride, okay? If I could, I'd take you now. We could disappear, just you and me. Would you like that?"

She nuzzles my hand begging me for another sugar cube, so I comply.

"I knew I'd find you in here."

Surprise has me spinning around at the sound of Blake's voice. The sun is shining at his back and it reminds me of the time I first saw him and I can't help but grin a little. He's wearing worn jeans that fit him perfectly with a white polo shirt and loafers. He looks handsome and my stomach immediately starts fluttering at the sight. How does he manage to always look so good? To make everything else around him disappear, pulling my entire focus to him?

"You were looking for me?" I ask.

He shrugs, "I know you well. When you have a lot on your mind, you tend to seek comfort here."

Feeling my cheeks flush, I shrug, "Busted."

"Are they good listeners?" He nods toward Cupcake and her neighbor Remy who's stuck his head out to greet Blake. Alternatively, he may merely be checking to see what the commotion is all about and what the likelihood is of stealing a treat. Blake smiles and gives Remy a sugar cube and begins rubbing his nose. I've never wished I was a horse before, even momentarily, until now.

"They're the best."

"I'm sure you're giving them an earful," he smiles at me.

"I had barely gotten started."

He turns to me, dropping his hand from Remy who makes a sound in displeasure at the loss of his attention. "I wish you'd talk to me instead. You haven't said much to me, or Jack."

"I guess I've... been processing everything. I don't mean to be distant."

"I know it will be weird with us not here, but it isn't like you'll never see us again."

"Don't speak logically to me, Blake. That doesn't help."

He grins, "What was I thinking?"

I shrug and turn away.

"What can I do, Sienna? What can I say?"

"Nothing. There's nothing you can do. It is what it is."

"Turn around and look at me."

Squeezing my eyes shut, I take a deep breath before I turn around and paste a smile onto my face. "Blake, I'm fine. Really. It just... took me by surprise is all."

His gaze roams over my face, I swear it pauses at my lips before his eyes connect with mine again. Wishful thinking I'm sure. "Why do I feel like that's not the whole truth?"

I smile, but it feels forced. "I wish-" I stop and bite my lip.

"You wish what?"

"I wish that you were having as hard a time about the fact that you're leaving, as I am."

His mouth opens to respond and I feel my face instantly flush embarrassed that I even voiced something so vulnerable. And I know I don't know exactly what all he is feeling about this change – likely he has mixed feelings but it's been hard for me to appreciate that. So, I wish I could snatch the words from the air and shove them back, never having voiced them at all because they don't matter and I'm making assumptions. Plus, at the end of the day, it doesn't change a damn thing.

"Sienna, I-"

Whatever he was going to say, never comes, because we're interrupted.

"Sienna?" My dad stops when he sees the two of us standing there. "Hey, Blake. Didn't know I'd find you in here too."

Blake nods and he looks as frustrated that our conversation was interrupted as I am.

"You better get in the house and help your mother. She's looking for you."

With a quick glance at Blake, I nod at my dad and swiftly exit and head to the house.

A few hours later, the party is in full swing. Laughter rings out through the air and our yard is full of people - high school students here to say their goodbye's as well as friends of my parents. I'm so glad mom and dad offered to have a joint party it felt like the right thing to do. And I'm fairly certain Blake's mom hadn't thought to celebrate with his friends - if at all - which is sad. I haven't even see her so I'm not sure if she's even here, but Mandy is and I'm thankful for that.

It feels like members of the whole town have come to shake Blake and Jack's hands and wish them luck. I've seen more than one person tuck some money into their hands, along with a pat on the back or a hug.

Conversation and laughter abounds; the smell of meat

cooking and barbecue permeates the air. There's a constant pop of a beer or soda can cracking open and people graze around the yard with full plates. Various lawn games are set up and I walk from person to person answering the dreaded questions I was trying to previously avoid.

"You must be so proud of your brother," Mrs. Thompson, one of my teachers at school says.

"Yes, of course."

"I'm sure you'll miss him, but what a great thing he's doing."

"It definitely is," I smile, "Oh, excuse me, I'm going to go grab another dessert from the kitchen."

I use that as an excuse to escape into the house. Seeing a pan of Rice Krispies on the counter, I cut myself a piece and munch in happiness while I avoid everyone.

"Rude," Vanessa says making me jump guiltily.

"God, you scared me! What's rude?"

"Cut me one too," she says holding her hands out and wiggling her fingers.

"I thought you had left already," I cut her a piece and hand it to her.

"Mom got sidelined by a friend on our way to the car. I saw you come in here and followed."

"I just needed to escape all the questions."

"I get it."

Taking the pan, I sit at the kitchen table and wordlessly cut us another chunk. We munch in silence.

"It will be okay, you know," Vanessa says quietly.

"I know. It will. Besides, I have you."

"Yeah you do, lucky bitch."

Laughing out loud feels good. She smiles at me but it falls immediately when we hear her mom yell her name.

"Gotta go!" She jumps up from the table and runs out

the door, suddenly stopping and turns around. "I'm lucky to have you too, you know." Before I can say a word, she disappears.

Heading back outside, I bring the marshmallow treats with me and place them on the table telling myself I don't need another one.

Laughter captures my attention and I look at one of the many tables to see Blake and Jack surrounded by their friends. I can't hear what Jack's saying from here, but he's gesturing wildly in his typical animated fashion and has the attention of everyone around him. I smile at his antics, laughing despite myself. That's the way he's always been - the life of the party - with Blake right along side him.

Suddenly, my heart sinks and the smile falls off my face. The happiness around me suddenly feels suffocating. Part of me wants to scream because I feel like they've forgotten me and moved on already, which makes no sense. My whole world feels like it's spinning out of control. The days since Blake and Jack told me their news have flown by and while I've tried to do my best to see it in a positive light and deal with my selfish emotions, waves of sadness still overwhelm me and I struggle - hard.

It's simple - I'm sad.

Part of me feels ridiculous that this is so hard for me. I want to - need to - get over it already.

During Jack and Blake's graduation yesterday, I was so proud watching them take the stage. I laughed with everyone when Jack of course did a stupid celebration dance upon getting his diploma and felt such delight as I watched Blake receive his. The huge grins on their faces were so genuine and the back slapping hug they gave each other was infectious.

Later, as they stood and smiled for photos at the insistence of my mother, they had their arms wrapped around each other's shoulders. A flash back of them hit me all at once. They were eleven, and had just won their first football game of the season. They had their helmets in their hands, were sweaty and filthy, and happy as can be after successfully sacking their opponents.

My mind quickly remembered them at thirteen, and the surprise invoked when they announced their intent to give soccer a try. They were standing together, giving the camera a thumbs up after Blake had scored three goals during the game, Jack two. I then recalled when they were sixteen, standing side by side next to Jack's new car, one he had bought off a used lot with money saved over the years from allowance and odd jobs, and with the help of our parents. Another picture for the album mom kept sacred like a religion. At each and every milestone I was there. Maybe not in the photo, but I was part of it, part of the moment. Through good times and bad – they were inseparable – and I was always included.

Watching then now, Blake walks up to Jack and stands next to him, showing him something on his phone. Seeing them side by side again, like always, it suddenly hits me hard that they will have many more moments together but I won't be a part.

It's not logical to feel this way.

Who knows what's going to happen when they go to boot camp - if they'll stay together after, where they'll end up - but it's still something they're doing together, another of life's landmarks they will pursue together.

But without me.

Reality once again sinks in and I feel an ache so deep inside my chest it feels like a huge chasm is going to swallow me whole.

Needing to escape, I turn and walk – almost run - in the direction of our treehouse.

Climbing inside, I sit in a chair so I can see out the window.

My thoughts race.

Shame vacillating with despondency hits me again.

Blake and Jack are always larger than life. Like tonight, they always have big smiles on their faces. But lately around me, they haven't. They've been quiet, knowing I've been adjusting to their news, even upset, and have graciously been providing me time and space to process how I feel. And while I know it's been a kindness, the atypical separation has created a distance between us that feels vast. It's huge- larger than I've ever experienced. Bigger than the time Jack and I made fun of Blake when he tripped in P.E. class in front of everyone and we reenacted it over and over. Even more than the time I didn't talk to the boys for days after they gave me crap because I still had my childhood doll in my closet - unable to part with her even though they said playing with dolls was stupid. Bigger than the time Jack got mad at Blake and me because we teamed up against him regarding a girl he had a crush on.

All childish things that seemed huge at the time almost make me laugh now. Those things were nothing compared to real life issues.

My mind dashing, I recall during one recent melt down in my room, my mom came in. She soothed me and spoke words of comfort but also told me that I would likely be happier if I dealt with how I was feeling quickly and enjoyed the time we had before they left. It was the only communication we've had on the subject, but she was right. The last thing I want is to have them leave with things feeling rocky, unsettled, unstated.

So I put on a happy face. I've been trying to save the grief and associated feelings for when I'm alone or with Vanessa.

I move from the chair and go sit at the side of the tree-house where my legs can hang down and swing back and forth. I feel mentally and emotionally exhausted. Putting on a show is not easy - I can see why actresses get awards for it. I almost laugh out loud at myself at the comparison.

"Sienna?" A voice calls from below startling me. "Sienna are you up there?"

"Blake?" I respond in surprise.

"I knew I'd find you up here." Funny...it's the second time in a few short hours he's known where to find me.

I hear his steps on each slat as he climbs higher and higher, I stand awaiting his arrival.

"Hey," he smiles when his head is poking through the hatch and is the only part of him visible.

"Um, don't you have a party where you're one of the guests of honor?" I tease.

He shrugs, "What are you doing up here?"

"Just needed to take a minute away."

"Ah," he says and climbs the rest of the way inside. He closes the hatch, turns toward me, and suddenly sways a bit.

"Whoa," I quickly grab his arm. "You okay?"

He smiles brightly, "I'm great. I think I just accepted a few more congratulatory drinks than I realized."

"Oh, I see," I laugh softly realizing he's just a little bit tipsy.

"Yeah," he laughs. He walks over to the window that faces his property. His face becomes serious.

"I'm sorry your mom couldn't attend tonight. At least I didn't see her. Is she working? Going to make it over later?"

He shrugs, "I'm not sure."

"Oh."

"How are you doing?" He asks.

"Blake, you don't need to keep checking on me. I'm fine. I will be fine. I know I've been... quiet and withdrawn, I was just... surprised, but I don't want you leaving and being worried about me. Your leaving isn't about me. And I'm so proud of you."

"I'll worry about you no matter what, Si."

"Well, it's not necessary. Really. You need to concentrate more on yourself and what you're about to do."

"Will you write to me?" He asks so softly that it takes me a moment to process his words.

"Yes, of course."

"I don't know if I'll have access to my phone often, or when, but maybe you can email me? I'll check it as often as I can."

"I can do that," I promise.

"Good. That's good," he nods, "I'd like that."

We're quiet as he looks out toward his property again.

"I started to tell you in the barn before your dad came in, that I'm going to miss you. You suggested that I won't, but that's not the case. You. Your family. Jack. You have become my family - my home."

Swallowing thickly, I nod.

"Do you remember the day we met?" He asks.

A smile comes to my face immediately, "How could I forget? I still have scars that remind me."

I can feel his gaze on my face, so I turn toward him. His gaze captures mine and his look is so intense, I lose my breath.

"Scars?"

"From when I fell. The one at my eyebrow. I also have one on the side of my lip from where a branch hit me on my way down."

His eyes immediately move to my mouth. "Is that where that's from? You're lucky you weren't hurt worse than you were."

I nod, but inside I'm thinking he noticed my mouth?

"You know, I'll never forget the first time I saw you," he almost whispers.

"You mean when I was flat on the ground and bleeding?"

He chuckles and the sound moving across me prickles my skin. "Who would have thought that you'd end up being one of the most important people in my life?"

Suddenly, he cups the side of my face and I lose my breath.

His eyes look deeply into mine. His thumb brushes the scar at the side of my mouth and before I can even prepare he places a kiss there.

I. Stop. Breathing.

He pulls away from me and stares into my eyes, almost like he's asking permission. I don't know what he sees in my face, I don't even know when I started breathing again, but his face starts to move to my own. My breath hitches, chills break out over my body, I feel his fingers flex against my face. All I can see are his lips coming toward my own. I close my eyes.

"Sienna? Blake?"

Blake jumps away from me at the sound of Jack's voice below.

My breaths are coming in and out so sharply, I'm afraid I'm going to hyperventilate.

Blake stares at me.

I stare back.

He swallows hard.

"Sienna? Blake? Are you guys up there?"

"Y-yeah," Blake calls clearing his throat and shaking his head.

Seconds later, Jack's head pops through the bottom of the treehouse as he pushes the hatch open.

He is completely unaware of the fact he's interrupted what was a life altering moment for me. And he has no idea that I want to scream, and tell him to get out. He has no idea that more than anything I want to jump into Blake's arms and plant my mouth on his and take what I've been longing for.

He places his arms around mine and Blake's shoulders and smiles, "Just where I want to be."

We spend the rest of the evening, just the three of us, ignoring the party as it comes to a close. We reminisce about games played, moments shared. We talk about places we want to go one day, things we want to do. The guys give me all kinds of advice on my last year in high school. I enjoy my time with them, but the entire time I keep replaying what happened between Blake and me over and over.

I wonder what could have been.

I wonder what would have happened.

I will likely never find out.

We're unlikely to ever be alone again.

At some point, we all fall asleep, awakening to Jack's alarm, reminding all that the moment is nearly upon us and they have a plane to catch.

I walk with them back to the house in silence.

Once they're ready, I watch as they gather their things.

I watch as they hug my mom goodbye; watch as she wipes her tears.

When it's my turn, I nod automatically when I'm asked to promise again that I'll write. When I'm asked to promise again that I'll take care of myself, and remember the advice they gave, I nod assent.

I hug them each tight.

I have a hard time letting go.

I watch as they get inside my dad's car.

I watch as the car moves down the driveway.

My gaze holds Blake's as he looks back at me, waving one more time.

I lift my hand to return the wave, and wipe at the tear that's fallen down my cheek.

That one tear turns into too many to count.

8

*I*t's been several months since the night in the tree house before Blake and Jack left. A night I replay over and over. Everything has happened – like the start of senior year of high school - and yet nothing feels truly significant. It's difficult not being able to share life with them. Sometimes I feel in suspended animation waiting for them and the life I was comfortable with to return, but I know that things have shifted and are forever changed. I move through life, but have great difficulty enjoying much of anything.

When I shake those thoughts from my mind I realize I'm smack in the middle of my senior year, and things are fine or I guess they are. I think I had it in my mind that my senior year would be this big unforgettable experience. I mean, I always knew it was going to feel strange without Blake and Jack, but it's altogether different than I had been planning for - they're not just away at college and won't be coming home for school breaks. And despite what I thought, I did not appreciate how much a part of my day-to-day life they were. It's not that we did everything together, but we frequently touched base, checked in with each other; cared about each other.

The house feels different without Jack. It's strange, I never realized how much of a presence he had, until he was gone. I miss things like hearing his steps in the hallway, his voice in the house, and I never thought I'd miss sharing a bathroom with him but even that's something I miss - seeing his stupid stuff all over the place. Truth is, it was there that we had some of our most poignant interactions. I don't know that I'd ever admit it, but I miss having his company at breakfast or when we would do our chores together. I guess the easiest way to explain it is that the house is simply much more quiet, and it feels like a part of me is missing. I'm not sure what he'd reply if I told him how I felt – would he tease me about hormones and ask if I'm on my period, or would he admit that he misses me too?

My mom and dad seem to be doing okay. There are moments when I see my mom get emotional. She always tears up when she receives an email or call from him. He texts when he can but that's not been too often. They were rarely allowed to use their phone or connect at all during training.

Since they left, they've only been back home once. It was after they finished boot camp. They were home for a few days before they had to leave again for more training due to assignments they received. I was so excited to see them both.

I saw Jack first.

He came storming into the house, "I'm home, bitches!"

He surprised us, we had no idea when he would be arriving. My dad and I laughed, my mom told him to watch his mouth before jumping up and hugging him and crying. Then he asked them for money to pay for the ride he arranged from the airport - typical Jack.

"Hey little sis," he'd said to me before pulling me into a hug which I returned

wholeheartedly. I'd be lying if I didn't admit I looked over his shoulder to see if he was alone.

As if he knew, Jack announced, "Blake will come by at some point."

"He's home too?" I ask and hope it sounds merely inquisitive, innocent.

"Yeah. He went to see his family."

It was a couple days before Blake showed up at our house. I gasped when he came through the door, and my heart flipped in my chest. He looked the same, but different in just the few months he'd been away. His cheeks looked sharper, his posture proper, and his skin was tanner like he'd spent a lot of time outdoors. He was definitely not hard on the eyes, but he never had been.

When he gave me a hug, it was obvious his body had seen some changes as well. I wanted to hang onto him longer than appropriate, and I may have even inhaled a bit with my face buried in his chest, but I tried not to be obvious about it.

I wanted to say so many things. I knew he'd gotten my emails since he'd replied when he could, but he'd never said a word to me about anything that had happened in the tree-house before he left. I sadly followed his lead and didn't say a word about it in my emails either. So our correspondence focused on military life and the trials and tribulations of boot camp. I wondered if maybe he wanted to wait until he saw me again in person - maybe being home, he would open up and we could talk about that. Perhaps we'd finally have a conversation about it and time permitting, I'm sure I could create an opportunity.

But it never did.

Aside from a night he had dinner with all of us, I never saw him at all. When he was here that one evening, we were never alone. It wasn't long before he and Jack were leaving again and I was once again waving goodbye while he was driving away.

I shed a few more tears with that departure, but it was better than the first time they left. I was beginning to accept the reality. The last time they left they had no idea when they'd be able to return.

The emails resumed and even escalated in frequency and checking to see if new ones had been delivered to my inbox has become an obsession. We talk about all kinds of things - how his advanced training's going, the things he misses about home, my grades, events at school, how the animals are doing on the farm. I give him updates on my parents, my friends - you name it. He will sometimes talk about some of the guys he's become friends with but it's nothing more than a mention here and there. He tells me about different places he's explored and things he's done on his down time. I devour every detail of his life. I take it all in and am thankful for the tidbits I get, even though we don't ever talk about anything I wish we'd talk about.

Okay, the *one thing* I wish we'd talk about.

Us.

Then, one night, that changes.

It's late and I'm still up working to finish an essay due the following day for history. Diving deep into the details about a postwar America, the sound of an email arriving in my inbox startles me, the sound reverberating loudly in my bedroom.

Immediately I switch screens and my heart begins to race when I see Blake's name in bold. It's not uncommon for me to receive emails from him late at night, but usually if he sees I'm on my computer at the same time, he'll instant message me. I don't know why, but I hesitate before opening the email.

Double clicking to open, I begin to read and the tone immediately feels different. Usually his emails begin with him asking what's new and exciting and then he tells me about his day and catches me up on whatever he can before asking me questions. But this time, he's immediately personal and direct.

Hello Sienna,

I see that you're online but I'm not brave enough to have a 'live' conversation with you. The guys and I went out tonight and I fear the few drinks I've had are making me bold. I think if I knew you were readily accessible on the other end, able to be in realtime with what I'm writing I wouldn't say this, and I want to say this. I want to tell you that you've been on my mind constantly. It's not just your emails, though they always seem to come when I need them the most - after a long hard day, or when I'm missing home the most - but it's more than that. I find myself often wondering things about you like how your day is going, sure, but it's more than that. It's thinking about the way you look when you smile. How your nose wrinkles in concentration when you're studying hard. The way your face lights up when you take care of the animals you love. The sound of your laugh when you're gossiping with Vanessa. My favorite though is the night of prom. Remember when we were driving you home? It was a beautiful night, but what was gorgeous was the sight of you during that drive. The windows down, the wind in your hair and on your face. You looked free, happy, content. It was beautiful. I think about that often when I feel homesick. They're things I have no right to think about, things I shouldn't think about, not ever. When I do, I usually push them into the back of my mind, burying them as deep down as I can. Tonight, the alcohol helps them float to the surface I think. So I'm letting them come. I'm exploring them, devouring them. I'm letting myself think about the color of your eyes, the curve of your lips, the feel of your skin when I touched your face that night in the treehouse. And Sienna, I'm letting myself wonder. I wonder what would have happened the night before I left. The night we were interrupted, and you know what? I'm letting myself need. I'm letting myself want. If it's wrong, I don't care. Not tonight. And I just needed to tell you that.

I stare at his email for a long time. I reread it more times than I can count. I even pinch myself to verify I'm not dreaming because there is no way, *no way,* that this is happening. I hit reply and only type a small reply.

Dear Blake,
    I think about it too.
    Yours,
    Sienna

That's all I say. I could go on and on but that just seems like enough. After I send it, I sit for a while, waiting to see if he responds. Part of me feels panicked and wonders if I should have waited, or said more, or let his words digest further before replying, maybe gotten Vanessa's advice first. But it's too late to take it back because in one word I had put my heart on the line. *Yours.* That word left nothing to wonder about how I feel.

It takes one whole week before he replies. Seven days of stress, doubt, and just plain freaking out. A week of constant email refreshing, checking on my computer, my phone, feeling sick to my stomach, second guessing and wondering how he perceived it, what he thought about it, if he'd even interpret in the manner it was intended. Maybe I hadn't said enough. His reply was short, but it held one hell of a punch. There was no room for misinterpretation of his intent.

Sienna,

If I could take that email back, I would. I'm so sorry, please forgive me. I can't lose you, not ever. You're my family. I let alcohol make me stupid and none of it even matters - it's too late now. Please, pretend it never happened.

Blake

Tears instantly fill my eyes. If it were possible to feel my heart break, I know I did. The pain in my chest is so intense, the sob in my throat immediate. Did I say something wrong? Kept it too simple? Had I left too much unstated? Had my response repelled him? Should I have let him know I thought about the moment often? Should I have confessed that I frequently close my eyes and still feel his hand touching my face, his lips at the corner of my mouth. I didn't tell him that the intensity in his eyes is forever imprinted in my brain and it's one of my most cherished memories; that I dream about him and spending time together and fantasize about what could have happened if only. I may be young but

I know how my heart feels. Perhaps he needed me to confess that I wanted to be his; that I would wait for him forever if he only said the word. In the end, I merely reply that there was nothing to forgive and I ask if we can please talk about his response I want so desperately to keep the opportunity open.

I never receive a response - not really. Instead his approach is to carry on the conversation as we had before - as if the interaction never occurred.

It breaks me.

Now, it's a month later.

And everything that happened before is the reason why I'm now dating. I realized my hope was just that - hope - and not supported by fact or substance. There's no reason to hope - all of it was nothing more than a girl's wish - a fantasy. When I pulled back and looked at it all as objectively as I could the last month, I actually felt embarrassed. It was past time I move on and let go. I had wanted to believe we could be together, but what proof did I have to support that? None. Nothing. Not one thing. I needed to stop reliving one stupid moment over and over because clearly, while I had thought it had meant the same thing to him as it did to me, it didn't.

So when Jesse asks me out for the third time, at Vanessa's urging, I finally say yes. Initially I thought of him a bit as my rebound, a chance to help me push Blake out of my mind, and decided that it was okay. But the truth is, we are having fun together. We've been on more than a handful of dates, alone and with others and we genuinely have a good time together.

Tonight, I'm going to his place. I'm meeting him there and we are going to have dinner together and watch a movie.

His parent's aren't home. We will be alone. I have a feeling things may escalate and while I feel nervous, I am willing to do whatever it takes to push Blake out of my mind once and for all and be open to other possibilities.

I'm nervous as I get ready, selecting my outfit carefully, taking great care with my appearance. I'm nervous when I drive to his house, nervous when he answers the door and places a soft kiss on my lips. We've already kissed, several times, and I like it. It makes me feel wanted, desired.

He's ordered take-out from my favorite restaurant and I can barely eat any of it. When we finally move to his family room and he puts a movie on, I don't even realize what it is we're supposed to be watching. I look at him, he turns and looks at me and before I know it, we're kissing.

It feels nice, the sensations running through me are pleasant. I know he's taken off guard when I pull him down on top of me. He hesitates and pulls away from me looking into my eyes in question and then for confirmation and approval. I put my mouth back to his and he kisses me fiercely. I squeeze my eyes shut and lose myself in the feeling of Jesse's body against mine, in the taste of his kisses. When his hands brush against my breasts and a place more intimate, I like the feelings it evokes.

Our intimacy progresses quickly. I remove his shirt, he removes mine. He pauses, "Sienna?"

"Hm?"

"What are we doing?" He asks with humor in his voice.

"I mean, if I have to explain this to you, it's a problem."

He chuckles, "Are you sure about this?" He pushes my bra strap down my shoulder and kisses it.

"Are you complaining?"

"No. Hell no."

"Then shut up and touch me."

I need this. I want to feel desired, wanted, needed by someone. On some level I know this is wrong. I know that this isn't who I really want to do this with; who I want to cause these emotions within me. The realization that I'm trying to fill the emptiness in my heart, in my soul, with something else mixes in with what I'm experiencing physically, but I can't choose to stop myself.

In no time, the rest of our clothes are gone. A condom has miraculously become available out of nowhere and I stare in wonder as he rolls it on himself. As he begins to push himself inside of me, I feel almost disembodied and as panic starts to rise in my chest, I tell myself it's okay, that I'm okay, that I want this, I need this.

There's a flash of pain and I grit my teeth.

A tear rolls down my cheek.

It's over fast. The most anticlimactic moment of my life.

I go to the bathroom and clean myself up quickly. It's when I glimpse myself in the mirror that I begin to become unraveled.

I take in my disheveled appearance. The glassy look in my eyes, the flush of embarrassment in my cheeks, the chapped state of my mouth, the dots of red on my throat and chest and I feel a heavy wave of shame rush over me and I begin to drown in it.

I fly out of the bathroom and grab my things.

"Sienna?"

I can't reply. There's a sob clogging my throat.

"Sienna, what's wrong? What did I do?" The concern in his voice calms me a little. The fact is, Jesse is a nice guy. A *really* nice guy. In a different time, a different life, I could see myself really liking him. If only I was able to let my heart be with someone else. Instead it's hung up on someone I will never have.

"I'm sorry, Jesse. I have to go."

"Wait," he grabs my arms. "I'm sorry. I thought you wanted-"

"I do... I mean, I did. You didn't do anything wrong."

"I know it was fast. I didn't mean to... I mean I shouldn't have..."

"It's not you, Jesse. I'm sorry. I have to go."

He calls my name but I'm out the door, in my car and driving away in record time. I cry all the way home. Sob. I hate myself. Hate that I'm so messed up that I'd resort to giving my first time to someone I don't love. Hate that I'm so wrapped up in Blake that his hot and cold attitude toward me is making me this out of control.

Jesse calls me several times over the next few days and tries to talk to me at school, but I break up with him giving him the worst excuse of all time, "It's not you, it's me."

I couldn't even blame him for laughing bitterly in my face.

I know he's confused. So am I. I have no doubt I've hurt him and I hate myself for it.

It's just that I have this small mustard seed of hope inside of me that Blake and I still have a chance. That whatever it is that drove him to send that original email has not evaporated and will keep insisting for recognition and acknowledgement, pushing at him until he breaks again. That he'll see that we are supposed to be together. He'll let go of this stupid notion that I'm off-limits. Because whether I like it or not, I am his, I will always be his.

I couldn't have been more wrong.

9

*I*t may be six o'clock in the evening, but the sun is still shining bright in the sky. It's only May, but here in Montana we start seeing the sun for twelve hours per day in March. The shade is cooler but of course our graduation ceremony is out on our football field, so there's no escaping the sun's warm rays. I look toward the bleachers on either side of the field with longing, wishing I could escape into the shade the awning above them creates.

A trickle of sweat falls down the back of my neck, the hair underneath my gold graduation cap feeling itchy. The school valedictorian drones on and on about our accomplishments, memories from years past and gives advice for our future. None of which anyone will remember later, I'm sure.

It was a long year. I did well, got great grades, went through the motions of immersing myself into the year as best I could. Looking to my left my gaze catches Jesse's. I instantly feel my cheeks heat with embarrassment, but he gives me a soft smile before turning away. He could have been awful to me after what happened between us, but all he's done is go out of his way to try and be my friend, only being upset with me initially. I apologized profusely for the way I behaved that night, but he brushed off each and every one repeatedly stating they were unnecessary. Rumors never circulated and the mortifying comments never came and as far as I know he kept it as quiet as I did. I didn't even tell Vanessa about the mistake I made that night.

A little beyond him, in the sea of gold and black, my gaze catches Vanessa's and she grins ear to ear. Even from here I can see the excitement sparkling in her eyes as she bounces in her seat eager to get this over. She's all about the after party - it's all she's talked about for days. A fellow senior by the name of Wes and his family offered to host the event. Their home resides on a large piece of land and we are having a dinner, bonfire, and live music to celebrate. It should be a good time and I'm looking forward to it too. I return Vanessa's smile and give her a wink.

It seems like forever, but when we finally line up and wait for our turn to walk across the stage, my heart races with excitement. Waiting to receive my diploma, the heat of the evening is forgotten while the last four years run through my mind like a slide show. There were hard times, sure, but there were also so many fun ones. I have no doubt that what I've learned during these four years and the moments that have helped me build my character will be appreciated later.

They finally call my name and the moment I walk across the stage feels like a blur. I hear my family cheering and yelling my name and I look out into the crowd and smile toward the direction of their voices since I can't see exactly where they're sitting.

The rest of the ceremony ends quickly and Vanessa and I immediately find each other and hug and squeal with excitement over the fact that we finally graduated high school. We began moving through the crowd looking for our families. Vanessa finds hers but I keep looking for my mom and dad's smiling faces.

"Sienna!" My name is called excitedly.

My head turns and I finally connect with my mom and dad.

"Congratulations sweetheart," my mom says with a wide smile on her face.

"Thanks."

"I'm so proud of you," my dad says and then suddenly hands a phone to me.

I look at him in curiosity and he nods encouragingly.

"Hello?"

"Hey, little sister."

"Jack!" My eyes instantly fill with tears - I so miss him.

"Sorry I can't be there in person. I hope to get home soon and when I do we'll celebrate together, okay?"

"Promise?"

"Of course. But hey?"

"Yeah?"

" I know it can't possibly be the same, but since I couldn't be there, I sent someone else in my place."

My heart. stops. beating.

"Wh-what?"

He laughs softly in my ear. "I couldn't get the time off, but someone else could."

It feels like it takes a minute for my brain to catch up to what my heart already knows. It starts beating rapidly and pounding so fiercely and loudly I am sure everyone else can hear it too.

Looking around, I don't know how I didn't see him before. My stomach twists in excitement and I feel tears burn the back of my throat. My lips speak his name without sound.

Beyond my parents a little ways, he stands proudly and a foot above everyone else. His lips are turned up in a soft smile, and something that resembles pride and excitement dance in his eyes.

He's really here.

He came for my graduation.

The phone is easily set aside as I mumble goodbye to Jack and thrust it into my dad's hands as I move past him.

People between us make a maze that I weave through to get to him. Our eyes never waver from each other as we walk toward each other in what feels like a slow motion scene from a movie. The smile on his face, the twinkle in the green eyes I love so much make my body sing. Like a magnet unable to move away from the pull of him, I keep moving closer as if I have no choice.

When we reach each other, I barely pause before I throw myself into his arms and he pulls me off my feet, spinning me around.

The past few months of hardly any significant words from him are forgotten - it all seems silly now that he's here.

"You're here," I say breathlessly while burying my face into his neck. I inhale. I can't help myself. I don't even stop to realize that my reaction to his being here screams my true feelings for him, but I don't care.

"Of course I'm here," he chuckles and his breath moves over my shoulder making me shudder. I'm suddenly aware of every place our bodies touch. My arms wrapped around his shoulders, my lips almost brushing the skin of his neck, my breasts pushed against his chest and our bodies lingering in places all the way down. I don't want to ever let go.

With great reluctance I pull away and he places me back on the ground. I look into his eyes with a big smile on my face. His smile returns mine, "I'm so proud of you. Glad I got to see you walk across that stage."

I shrug feeling embarrassed, "It's not a big deal."

He reaches out and tugs the cords indicating that I graduated with honors, and shakes his head, "Yes it is. And how about the fact you're going to Montana State?"

"It's really not a big deal," I shrug again embarrassed that I'm staying in state when I always imagined I'd go far away for school. Fact is, I was going to get more scholarship money by staying local.

"Stop saying that. You're amazing. And like I said, I'm proud of you."

"How long do we have?" I ask and my throat clogs up immediately knowing that our time is likely limited. "Until you have to leave?"

He smiles sadly, "I only had a couple days - have to head back to the airport shortly."

I frown confused, "A couple days, but you're leaving today?"

How is it that I can feel so happy and sad at the same time. Suddenly, I feel like now is my chance. Who knows when I will get to see him again. And I'm tired of the hot and cold - after his confusing email, there's so many things I'd like to say. Maybe now is my chance before he leaves. I can make my feelings clear. I want to tell him. Tell him I've loved him since the day I first saw him. I'm done pretending what I feel isn't real.

"Blake? Are we going to leave now? You have to get to the airport."

Confusion washes over me and for a moment I don't understand who's speaking. My brow furrows and I look at

Blake in confusion before I see an arm slink through his, long red nails gripping the skin at the inside of his elbow.

Realization crawls over me like spiders racing across my skin. The hair on the back of my neck and my arms stands on end and my stomach drops. Tears instantly burn my eyes, but this time it's a feeling besides joy making them appear.

He's here, yes. But he's here with *her*.

How is this happening?

Something in his eyes change and I can't nail down the emotion in them.

"Hailey?" I say her name, the uncertainty in my voice clear. Her graduating a year early was the best thing to ever happen. I haven't seen her since.

"I told you to wait for me," Blake says, his gaze still on me.

"I know, but it was taking forever and it's hot. We only have a little time left, so I wanted to come and get you so we can have a proper goodbye. Are you ready?"

"Go back to the car, I'll be there in a minute, okay?"

My gaze flies between them as they talk, but when she smoothes her hand over the front of her dress, something inside of me dies as realization rips through me.

There's a small bump at her stomach. I squint at it for a minute, then my eyes fly back to hers. The look of triumph on her face is all the affirmation I need.

This can't be happening. For a brief moment I wonder if this is all a joke or a dream. I pinch the skin inside my arms when I cross them, but nope, it's real and it's standing before me.

The world suddenly grows fuzzy. It's like everything has suddenly become pixelated and I can't see anything or anyone clearly. A buzzing begins in my ears and I vaguely realize I'm in shock as the words from his email suddenly repeat over and over in my mind, "*It's too late now.*"

It takes me a full minute to realize he's saying my name over and over again. I want to reply, but I can't seem to get my mouth to form the words. I'm simply staring at him without responding.

He takes my shoulders in his hands and I immediately shake them off, "Don't touch me."

His brow furrows with worry and something that looks like hurt. Oh the irony. I could laugh out loud, "Sienna?"

A funny thought enters my head and I finally do laugh and I'm positive the sound is partly hysterical. Is he expecting me to be happy for him? For them? How can he not know? He has to.

"Sienna, what's wrong?" My dad asks, his hand landing on my shoulder making me jump a little. His question brings clarity back to me and as I turn and see my parents. I blink several times. When my gaze catches my mom's it almost makes me choke on a sob. There's knowledge deep within, she's known all along how I feel. Everyone else may be clueless, but not her, never her. She takes a half step toward me, then stops and looks around. I can see she's internally battling whether or not to gather me in her arms.

"Mom, dad, I love you. I'm going to go to that party with Vanessa and I'll see you later, okay?"

My dad smiles and nods and takes my mom's hand. They say something and walk away, my mom looking at me uncertainly and I nod at her and try to smile.

Vanessa is suddenly in sight. She's standing with her parents and mine speak to hers on their way out. Her eyes are full of concern and sadness for me. She says something to her parents and then she's with me, her hand in mine squeezing. A silent reminder she's there for me.

I half turn to Blake, "Thanks for coming. Have a safe trip back. Excuse me."

Moving as quickly as I can, the need to get away overwhelms me. "My car is over here," Vanessa says and leads the way.

Everyone I pass is a blur, there are calls of congratulations as I pass, people asking me if they'll see me at the party. I nod absently and keep moving, unable to respond more than that.

Reaching the parking lot, I see her car ahead and full on run. I can feel a sob bubbling in my chest and an ache flows through my body so hard and sharp it feels like its own entity.

Yanking on her car door handle I realize she hasn't unlocked it yet. I put my head down and breathe deeply waiting. I hear a click just as there's a hand on my shoulder pulling to turn me around.

Blake. He's followed me and stands staring at me, his breaths coming fast, eyes looking wild.

"Sienna, what's wrong?"

I laugh, "Did you really just ask me that?"

He looks down and back at me again, "I was going to tell you."

"Oh my god, I can't do this right now."

"Why did you run away? You look like you're going to cry. I'm sorry I hadn't told you yet. It was a shock-"

Staring at him standing before me, the light from the setting sun hits his dark hair making it shine like a dark halo. His concerned eyes are wide and green, and in a flash I'm reminded of the day we met, the memories flashing through my mind once again, one after another like they have a million times before. It makes my chest ache so hard that I gasp for breath.

"Stop! Just stop. I don't want to hear it. I'm so done caring. Just, leave me alone."

"What do you mean? Why are you so mad? I don't understand."

"How are you so oblivious, Blake?"

"Oblivious to what? Why do I feel so stupid?"

"You're not stupid! *I'm* stupid! Because after all this time you'd think that I would have known that loving you was just plain stupid."

"What do you mean? I love you too, Sienna. I'm sorry I didn't tell you about this. Like I said, it wasn't expected. The last time I was home, I guess it happened and then she sent me a letter-"

"Stop."

"Stop?"

"I don't want to hear anymore. It doesn't matter. Just go, Blake. Go back to Hailey and get to the airport."

I'm aware of the fact that Vanessa is standing there looking like she doesn't know what to do. I ignore her, not caring what she's witnessing.

"I don't want to leave like this. Tell me why you're so upset."

"Would you just stop it!" I scream, my anger making fire run through my veins.

"Stop what?" Blake asks looking confused and taking my shoulders again which I immediately brush off.

I laugh. I laugh and I can't stop. Gasping for breath, holding my belly, I ask, "How could you not know? You *have* to."

"Know what?"

"But it doesn't matter," I keep speaking as if he never did. "It never has. You don't see me. I'm no one to you and in the meantime I just keep getting hurt over and over and over again. When will I learn?"

"Don't see you? All I've ever seen is you, Si. You're my best friend too. More than my best friend. You're everything."

"Everything?" I laugh. "Then how could you be with her?" My voice breaks. "Are you....are you not attracted to me?"

His face falls, he shakes his head, "Sienna," he whispers my name.

"I love you," I confess and it feels like I've dropped a bomb between us. Even Vanessa gasps because she knows this is it. This is more than the usual I love you's we've exchanged before. "I've been *in love* with you for as long as I can remember and all it brings me is pain."

"Sienna, I-"

"No. Don't say anything. I already know. You're my brother's best friend. I'm like a little sister. Believe me, I know. I've reminded myself of that over and over through the years. Each time I could swear that you saw something or felt something toward me too, I reminded myself that it wasn't real. I know it isn't, but I just can't stop."

"Blake?" I hear *her* say his name again and I let out a sob at the sound.

"Hailey, I'll be at the car in a minute."

"Just go," I tell him quietly at first.

"Sienna please," he says and I hear the pain in his voice and it angers me.

"Just go!" I turn around and scream at him. His eyes widen and his mouth falls open in surprise. "I can't do this anymore. I won't. I need to move on. I need to let go. I need to stop hurting all the time. Just go, Blake. Clearly, you have other things that are much more important. I can't do this anymore," I repeat.

"Sienna, no, don't do this, we need to talk..."

"No, we don't."

"Blake, what's going on?" Hailey asks again her gaze bouncing back and forth between us.

I laugh bitterly and finally pull Vanessa's car door open and get inside closing the door. Vanessa is already inside and the car is running - I don't know when that happened, but I'm grateful. "Can we please go? Now?" She nods.

Blake knocks on the window, "Please roll down the window, Sienna."

Looking into his eyes, I see the sadness and pain there that I know I've caused, but I can't find it in myself to care. The vast hole in my chest requires too much of my attention instead of focusing on any pain I may have caused him.

When Vanessa starts to drive forward, Blake calls my name again, walks with the car, and knocks on the window frantically.

I look away and doing so I swear I feel a sharp pain in my chest that has to be my heart breaking.

My eyes close and a tear rolls down my cheek as we drive away, Vanessa's hand finds mine and squeezes.

I swear I hear him yell my name as we drive away.

Blake tries to email me several times after that day.

He tries to call a couple times too.

I shut down my email address, change my phone number and make Jack and my parents promise to never share any information about me with him or vice versa.

I know that as painful as it is, it's what I need.

Jack questions me like crazy, but I don't give him anything until a couple years later when he's home and we're drunk and it all comes spilling out. How I felt, how I hurt, and why I needed to let go. He nodded, squeezed my hand and we never spoke of it again. I have no clue if he even remembers the conversation, but I think the pain in my voice and eyes was sobering enough for the both of us. Not sure he can forget it even if he wanted to.

There were times over the years I missed Blake desperately or wondered if I'd done the right thing. I never spoke to him again and sometimes the pain of missing him felt unbearable, but over time it became easier. Whenever the hurt became too much, I reminded myself the pain that came with hanging on - and it was far worse.

I let the memory of him become an echo that became softer and softer with time.

10

Seven Years Later

"I'm so sorry that happened Ms. Campbell, but it's definitely a risk of treatment. That's why it's listed in the consent form you signed. It should clear up in a day or two, but if it gets worse give us a call, right away, okay?"

"Thank you, I'm just really concerned about this, dear. I'll keep an eye on it."

"Alright, you take care now," I wave as she walks out the door then turn to my business assistant. "Let's follow up with her in a couple days and make sure she's okay, alright?"

"No problem," Tracie nods.

"It's literally the size of the point of a pen," I shake my head. "I had to almost squint to see it," I shake my head at the patient worried about a small burn she received on her gums from the teeth bleaching she received.

"I feel really bad, I took all the necessary precautions," my hygienist Kerry worries.

"I know you did, it's ok. That can happen, it's why its in the consent form. We'll follow up like I said and I'm sure she'll appreciate that. Don't worry about it."

Returning to my office I pull up my email and take a look at all the emails that managed to come in while I was speaking to the patient and observing patient care around the office.

Saying my life hasn't exactly gone the way I expected is an understatement. There are times when that makes me sad, but other times I know that doors had to close for others to open. My job being one of them.

A couple years into my college education we lost my mom to a sudden heart attack. It was heart-wrenching and her loss will never be something I recuperate totally from. When she passed, Jack could only take a short leave. He arrived only a day ahead of her services. He helped with final preparations and then assisted with chores and taking care of some things at the house that dad had clearly not had time to manage. Moreover, it was clear that dad needed... someone.

I knew it needed to be me.

Against his wishes, I dropped out of college and moved back home for a little while to help him manage the house, the animals and the field. He just needed someone to get him through and help make some difficult decisions.

A couple years after that it was past time for me to get my own place and my own job. My dad paid me for my help, but I was way past needing to be on my own.

Our local dental office, Mason Creek Dental, was looking for an assistant and I applied. The manager at the time, Theresa, hired me during our interview and thus began a new and unexpected career in dentistry. It was slow going and at times I wondered what I was thinking and if I was in over my head, but each week and month it became easier and easier. Before I knew it, five years later I was promoted to Practice Manager when Theresa was promoted herself.

My career may have been unexpected, but I love it and at times felt like it was made for me. Customer service and managing our team comes easy to me, maybe it's because I feel like I'm genuinely helping - that I have something to offer in helping people whether it's in ensuring they receive the best possible service and care or assisting and encouraging others in reaching their optimal potential. It's rewarding and challenging in the best way.

The practice is successful, I have a great team and it's an honor and privilege to work there each day. I still help my dad as needed, but he's doing great and has his own help with anything he needs; he doesn't really need me as much as before. He still misses my mom a lot, but he's done well for himself over the years. He's even dating again.

Speaking of which, I look at my watch and see it's about time for me to leave for the day. I'm meeting my dad and his girlfriend, Meghan for an early dinner.

"Sienna?"

"Yes?" I ask turning to find one of my new dental assistants Shari standing in the doorway of my office.

"Can you show me where I need to go to sign up for that training you were telling me about?"

"Sure," I smile and gesture for Shari to come stand at my computer while I explain how to manage our training platform.

My leaving is delayed by a few more questions from other team members, and I'm racing to meet my dad. On the way, my phone rings and my car phone shows a call coming in from Vanessa which makes me smile.

"Hello?"

There's garbled noise when I answer and then I hear, "No, Sam! Stop putting the dog's tail in your mouth. It's not a chew toy."

I can't help but laugh, "V?" I call wondering if she meant to call me or if it was an accident.

"Yeah, hey, sorry. As soon as you picked up, your godson put Murphy's tail in his mouth again."

"Well they do say that babies will put anything in their mouth at that age."

"Drives me crazy."

"How are you? Do you need a break? Where's Scott?" I ask referring to Vanessa's husband. They met in college and had a whirlwind romance. They were married soon after graduating and Sam was already a one year old. He was the happiest baby I've ever seen - he started walking early – at about ten and a half months - and he's into everything. Scott's an accountant and given that it's tax season he's working a lot of hours. Vanessa worked as a teacher for a little while, but once Sam was born, she decided she wanted to stay at home with him full time.

"Oh, I'm fine. He'll be home soon. It's just amazing how fast that kid can move for being so small. And he's into everything."

"I'll come spend some time with him this weekend and you can go get a pedicure or something."

"A pedicure? Forget that. My toes be damned. I'll take a nap instead."

"Sounds like a deal," I laugh.

"Hey, I remember you're having dinner with your dad tonight, but I heard something and wanted to give you a heads up."

"Okay, what's up?"

"I was at the market earlier. Alana was working and checked me out because one of the other cashier's was on break. Anyway, she told me that when she was at Sal's Meats getting some stock that she ran into Bess, our town's dispatcher and-"

"Oh my gosh, Vanessa. I know who Bess is and I don't need the whole entire low down on where the gossip you're about to tell me came from. Just spit it out."

She hesitates, "Okay..."

My stomach turns a little at the hesitation in her voice, "What?"

"Virginia Walker passed away," she says so quickly I'm not sure I heard her correctly.

"What?"

"Mrs. Walker, Blake's mom, passed away."

"Oh no..." my mind begins to spin. It's been a long time since I've seen her. She may still live next door to my dad, but she kept to herself and honestly the stories I heard about her various drinking escapades were the only news I ever really heard.

"Yeah, so Bess said that she heard that the medical examiner-"

"Vanessa," I say her name impatiently knowing she was about to go through the whole list again of how the news traveled. One of the annoyances of living in a small town.

"Oh, sorry. I guess she was dead for a little while before someone found her. She didn't show up to a doctor appointment and word traveled when there was another appointment she didn't make either and anyway they went to check on her and found she'd passed. No doubt she finally managed to drink herself to death."

"No doubt," I murmur. The antics of her drinking never faded over the years. Sadly I think people just became used to hearing about it. She'd lived alone for years now. Mandy long since left Mason Creek and I lost track of her and Blake... well Blake has never come home that I've heard.

"I just wanted to tell you because your dad may mention it and well because-"

"Because?" I ask when she stops mid-sentence.

"Well, do you think Blake will come home?"

My hands tighten on the steering wheel at the thought, "I don't know. I suppose it's possible. I certainly hope he gets to pay his respects. It would be the right thing, but who knows."

I hear her sliding glass door open and she says something to Sam about building a sand castle in his sand box before she asks, "How does that make you feel?"

"I have no idea," I admit. "I want to say it has no impact but in truth, I need time to process."

"That's understandable. I still can't believe he didn't come back when your mom passed."

"Yeah well, it's not always easy to just take leave when you want, you know that. He did send a beautiful floral arrangement which was nice."

"I remember, but I stand by what I said."

I chuckle at my loyal friend, "I appreciate the heads up. Now when my dad or someone else mentions it I'll be prepared."

"Yeah, that's what I was thinking. Sam! No! What did mommy tell you about eating grass?" I hear the phone fumble around and maybe hit the ground and her voice rings out, "I'll call you later! Sorry! Sam!"

I laugh and hang up the phone.

Pulling into the parking lot to a restaurant that my dad loves in the town next to ours, I hurriedly make my way to the entrance. When I walk inside I'm instantly greeted, "Hello, love."

"Jesse, hi. How was your day?"

Jesse, yes *that* Jesse, and I have been dating for a year. We ran into each other at the market and got to talking. Next thing I know he asked me to dinner and I accepted. I was nervous after what happened between us years before, as some memories linger longer than others, but once I got past that, we actually had a good time together. He's been asking me for months to move in with him and I keep finding a reason as to why it's just not the right time yet. I haven't really taken the time to explore why I'm so hesitant but he's been patient, even if persistent.

"It was good," he smiles before putting his arm around me and leading me through the restaurant. "They're already seated, I said I wanted to wait for you to arrive."

"Thank you, that was kind of you."

He pulls me close and kisses me on the head, "Of course."

When we arrive at the table, my dad stands and hugs me. "Hi honey."

"Hi, dad. Hi Meghan."

"Hello, dear. How are you?"

I smile and nod. I usually meet my dad for dinner or lunch or something every couple of weeks as I can. Work keeps me pretty busy but we meet and I go by the house periodically.

We've barely ordered and already the news Vanessa warned me about gets brought up by Meghan.

"It's just so sad. I really hope that I don't die alone. That's awful. Just awful."

"You should probably call and let Jack know, dad," I tell him.

"Why would he want to know?" Jesse asks curiously.

"Because Blake is his best friend and his mother just died," my dad replies.

"Oh that's right. I guess I didn't realize Jack and Blake still talk, let alone are still best friends."

"Why wouldn't they?" I ask.

"No reason," Jesse smiles and shrugs.

"I already sent him a text," my dad says with a grin.

"Look at you!" I praise knowing he's the least tech savvy person I know.

Our food arrives before long and I'm in the middle of listening to my dad tell me about the mare that's expecting her baby any time and how he's excited for its arrival.

Suddenly, Jesse turns to me and says, "So, I have an announcement to make."

"You do?" I ask turning to him with surprise having no idea what he's referring to.

"Yes. I was offered a job position in Oregon, one I can't possibly turn down, and I want you to come with me, Sienna."

I choke on the bite I've just placed in my mouth, "Excuse me?"

"I love you," holy hell, he chooses dinner with my father and his girlfriend to tell me this: To ask me to move away? "And I want a future with you. Say you'll come with me."

I don't think this could get more awkward until I look at my dad and see his mouth is wide open in shock with surprise consuming his face.

"Jesse, I uh don't know what to say," I respond, but the truth is I do know what to say. My insides are screaming no, but I don't want to say that in front of everyone.

"Say yes. Say you want a future with me too."

"I, um,-"

I'm saved from answering when my dad's phone suddenly beeps.

I can't help but smile a little when he composes himself, and places his glasses at the tip of his nose so he can peer at the screen.

He clears his throat and looks at me, " "It's Jack," he says.

"Yeah? Tell him he owes me a text," I instruct him yet very aware of Jesse's agitation at his moment being interrupted. And that he is still waiting for my answer.

"He says that he's coming home," he smiles.

"He is?"

"Yes."

"Okay, that's great, but back to my moving, Sienna, and you coming with me," Jesse interjects and I sort of want to punch him.

"Jesse, I need some time to think about that, okay?"

"Oh. Yes. Sure. Of course. Okay," he seems crestfallen and I seriously wonder at his common sense. Was he really expecting me to jump up in excitement and scream yes? My job is here, my dad, Vanessa. How did I not know he's insane? "I guess I did spring that on you, huh?" He laughs but it sounds hollow.

"We'll talk later," I tell him. I quickly see our conversation from a different perspective. Perhaps I've been a bit naïve, and certainly not fully attuned to the extent of Jesse's feelings for me. Why else would he have risked this here and now?

"Yeah," my dad clears his throat and I'm thankful he's steering the conversation away from this train wreck. "Jack's due some time off and is coming home for Virginia's funeral so he can be with Blake."

I nod and smile but it feels frozen on my face. I knew Blake would likely come home after I heard the news, I mean, I have no idea what kind of relationship he's kept up with his mom over the years if at all, but I imagine there's some things he needs to handle.

I just never expected that one of those things would be me.

11

_M_y stress level is currently a thirteen out of ten, easily. It's the day of the funeral and Jack asks me to attend with him. I had planned on going anyway, it's the right thing to do, but I readily agree. I've been flat out panicking since then about seeing Blake again.

Blake.

I can't help but wonder how he's doing. How he's dealing with the passing of his mother and my heart hurts for him because I know for a fact his mom continued to have an alcohol abuse problem until her death. I recall vividly how Blake felt about that and I can't imagine it made a reconnection likely, but who knows. At least I'm assuming because he's never been home - at least that I know of. I'm confident I would have heard though.. This town reveals every secret eventually I swear. And Blake is now known as one of the town's military heroes. So yeah, I would have known if he was ever back before today.

Especially since now it's all anyone in town seems to be talking about.

I actually snapped at some employees at work this week

telling them to gossip less and take care of patients more. I felt bad for a few minutes knowing that it was the subject of the gossip that was really getting to me, but oh well, I'm human too.

The information I have about what Blake's been up to over the years is minimal. Despite my requests to not tell me much, things still circulated. I know that he's not with Hailey, but I don't know how or why or even if they had a boy or girl - her family moved away a while back except for her brother and he's not one for gossip, so I haven't heard a thing. I do know that Blake lives in California as does Jack. They were both stationed there and have lived there ever since. Jack has invited me out to visit him several times over the years, but I've always come up with an excuse because I didn't want to chance seeing Blake. It's ridiculous to still be like that all these years later, I realize that, but the truth is that I've never really gotten over him.

It's why I've never taken things to the next level with Jesse or any man I dated prior to him. I compared them all to Blake which perhaps is both pathetic and unfair. We never had anything. I see that clearly now. It was all just a stupid girl crush, a significant and deep one from my perspective, but the truth is the feelings I had for him, the way seeing him or talking to him made me feel was far more impactful than even I can believe at times, and certainly far more meaningful than what Jesse or anyone else made me feel.

Jesse.

His announcement at dinner took me more than a little off guard. In the days since he's wanted an answer and has sent me information about Oregon and the area we'd live in an attempt to try to lure me further. I confess that part of me has been considering it. I've always wanted to visit Oregon, and I mean, Jesse loves me. I think I could be happy with him - he's a good man. But is that enough?

In truth, the other part of me, perhaps the more honest and wise part, knows that since my immediate reaction to his invitation wasn't a resounding 'yes, absolutely' and that I truly had no heartfelt desire to go anywhere with him - hell I didn't even want to move in with him – that clearly being with him, being together, is not a decision that would be true to my heart. So why am I postponing telling him? Truth is, things with Jesse have likely run their course and I need to tell him so. It's just that he's been so kind and I kept telling myself that maybe with time, my feelings would change. But that's not going to occur. And I know that is the truth. It would be unfair to keep him waiting longer. I'm not sure why it took him asking me for this commitment for me to confront the truth, but different situations require different catalysts, I've learned.

Walking into the funeral home where the service will be held before we head to the grave site, I do my best to push these thoughts aside for now. I take a moment to look down at myself and smooth my black dress making a final appraisal. It seems quite vain given the circumstances, but I'm incredibly aware that this is the first time I'll see Blake in years. I know the years have been kind, I still look relatively the same – in fact, mainly even better - but I allow myself a moment of insecurity before I brush it off, push my shoulders back and lift my chin.

Jack immediately comes into my line of sight. As if he knows what I'm thinking he looks at me with a smile before approaching me, crooking his elbow out for me to link my arm through, "You look great," he says and I could hug him.

"Well, you look handsome," I tell him. He does in his

dress blues. He's going to make some girl very happy one day.

"I've missed you," his eyes turn sad. "What will it take for you to come visit me?"

I feel bad immediately, "We can talk about it."

"Really?"

"Yeah. I'm sorry. I just..."

He's kind giving me an excuse, "I know work keeps you busy and aside from that you've been a rock to dad when I haven't been able to be. And have I told you thank you for that? It won't be long and my commitment will be done and I'll be able to be around more, help more."

"It's okay, Jack. I've always understood that."

"Doesn't mean it's been easy for you and I know that."

"Thanks for saying that."

"Oh and we also need to talk later," he says.

"About what?"

"What is this I hear about your being asked to move away?"

"Oh god, dad told you."

His eyes are shining with humor, "Shut up," I tell him. "We'll talk about that later too." He squeezes his arm closer to his body which pulls me closer - a hug of affection which I wholeheartedly return.

As soon as we walk into the funeral home, the smell of lilies is overwhelming. There are already several people lingering around the reception area speaking in hushed tones. There are some core members of Mason Creek that would die before missing an event of any kind - including a funeral. If you ask me it's because the information they'll potentially gain from the event will help sustain their gossip needs for days afterward. Not to mention they just want to be able to say they were there when whatever may happen happens. God forbid something were to transpire and they'd miss witnessing it in person. Small town life can be wonderful, but that's the part I could do without.

We weave in and out of people constantly getting stopped by people wanting to greet Jack, happy to see him and ask how he's doing. Some things never change - like their love for my brother. It makes me smile at how much his attention is sought and the fact that he's always cordial and kind. I suppose that's one of the reasons he's loved so much.

When we walk into the main room where the casket is at the front of the room and chairs are set up for the service, I immediately see Blake standing at the front of the room. My heart begins beating triple time and I gasp quietly at the sight of him.

Time has been kind to him as well.

Same dark hair of course, but instead of the buzz cut that he last sported, it's grown out. I can see tracks that indicate he's been running his hands through it over and over - an old habit that brings an easy smile, a little familiarity. Strong chin, cheekbones and full lips. He's got a furrow between his brow as he listens and nods to whomever he is speaking. He's got a new accessory too - glasses - and my god they only make him look more attractive.

My chest tightens at the fact that we're in the same room after all these years. I feel like I can't breathe.

"Excuse me," I mutter to Jack before leaving the room and heading to where the sign says there are restrooms. I know I need to hurry, people are making their way into where the service will be held and the last thing I want to do is walk in after its already started and make a spectacle of myself.

Quickly walking to the sink, I look at myself in the

mirror and see how wide and panicked my eyes look. My face has no color and I pinch my cheeks in an effort to create it. Taking some deep breaths I grab a paper towel, wet it and pat the back of my neck. Thankfully I'm alone so no one hears me talk to myself, "You can do this. It's not about you. It's about respect. And being here for Blake. And Mandy. Our history doesn't matter."

With another deep breath, I throw the paper towel in the trash, tug my purse up higher on my arm, walk out of the bathroom and smack right into someone.

"Oh, I'm sorry," I mutter into a firm chest.

Arms come to the sides of my arms steadying me. When I pull back I look up and right into the eyes of Blake. Of course. It's like a freaking movie.

"Blake."

"Si," he says using my nickname and it almost breaks me. Almost.

We stare at each other for a moment and then I'm in his arms hugging him tightly. "I'm so sorry," I tell him.

"For what?" He asks and his tone sounds tight.

I pull back and look into his face and there's so many emotions there - all of them indefinable. He's not smiling, just staring at me intently and the sight throws me out of whack.

He's wearing his dress blues and my god does he look handsome. He appears bigger than life. His chest is broader, he seems taller though I know it's just from not being around him for so long. His jaw is tight and I can tell he's clenching it while he awaits my response.

I step back working hard to control myself. I swallow several times my mouth feeling dry, "I'm sorry about your mom."

"Oh. Is that all you're sorry for?"

"Excuse me?" My stomach sinks and the fire in his eyes makes me lose my breath.

"I'm sorry to interrupt, but Mr. Walker? We're ready to begin."

He nods with a quick jerk of his head "Thanks." When he turns back to me his eyes fall to my mouth before they meet my eyes again. "Sienna," he says my name again with a nod before turning to walk away.

"Wait," I say and he stops and looks at me. Suddenly I realize this isn't the time or place. "Never mind. We can talk later."

"Oh, we're talking now?"

"Blake-"

"Later." He walks away and when he does, I'm startled to see he moves with a slight limp. I can do nothing but stare after him before I follow and slide into the spot behind my brother which of course happens to be directly behind where Blake sits with his sister, Mandy.

I do my best to pay attention, but my mind keeps going over our interaction again and again. He's angry and should I be surprised? I cut him off years ago, never giving him the chance to speak to me again. I'm not sure what I should have expected.

The service was okay, but it was really hard seeing Mrs. Walker lying there, makeup caked on her face trying to make her look better in death than I remember ever seeing her look in life. The funeral brought back memories of my own mother's and it made me emotional. Jack held my hand tightly and I know his thoughts were aligned with mine.

After the funeral ends, we take Jack's car to the gravesite and the service there is brief. Looking across the coffin, I see that Mandy stands next to Blake. She has tears silently falling down her cheeks while Blake looks stoically at the casket. As if he feels me watching him, his gaze meets my own. He holds it for a moment, before he looks away.

When it's over, Jack escorts me back to his car. "There's going to be a gathering at Blake and Mandy's house. We should go."

"Okay," I nod in agreement wanting yet dreading another chance to talk to Blake.

When my phone buzzes in my purse I take it out and see I've got a text from Jesse asking me if I've made a decision yet. Irritation rises in me at his insistence and I know without a doubt that I need to stop pushing this off any longer.

My text back is short and to the point, "Jesse, I'm sorry. I can't go. My dad's here, my job...I'm sorry. You deserve someone in your life that would immediately say yes and would give up anything and everything to be with you - I'm not that person. Forgive me." Do I feel bad that I texted him back my reply, yes, but he did ask me on text.

I feel worse when he responds, "I understand."

He's a good man, but that's why I know he deserves someone better than me. I know I made the right decision. I spent less than five minutes standing in front of the restroom interacting, if that's what I can call it, with Blake and the feelings that ran through me from seeing him again were far stronger than the feelings Jesse and our relationship ever managed to invoke.

Seems I'm simply doomed to love Blake forever. Even after all this time.

*a*fter all this time, the Walker's house still looks the same. It seems that updating things wasn't a top priority of Virginia Walker. I hadn't been inside their house too often, Blake had always preferred to come to ours, but the nostalgia still hits hard.

The house is full of people and the smell of the various casseroles offered in condolences is overwhelming. Dad and Jack are both here and I place the pie I made on the table to join all the other gifts. Blake and Mandy will have food for days. I wonder how long they're both staying.

Looking around I see Blake has changed his clothes. No longer in his dress blues he's wearing jeans and a blue button down rolled up at the sleeves. Ink peeks out under a sleeve of one of his arms making me curious about the tattoos he's obviously gotten.

He's speaking with Mrs. Gilderoy, one of our teachers from grade school. She's hanging onto his arm and he's smiling softly at her and nodding his head. A feeling of affection runs through me and I smile at the sight despite the circumstances surrounding it.

Various individuals come and talk to Jack too and I stand by listening and nodding and smiling when necessary, the whole time aware of where Blake is in the room, who he's speaking to and what he's doing. At one point Jack and I are alone and he catches me watching Blake as he steps outside. I consider going after him but I'm sure he could use a moment alone.

"Have you spoken to him yet?" Jack asks and I was so involved in my thoughts it makes me jerk a little and then I laugh at my jumpiness.

"Briefly. It, uh, it didn't go well."

"I can imagine it didn't."

I turn and look at Jack full on, we've never spoken about Blake directly over the years other than one time we were both drunk and I over-shared. Jack was smart enough to know there was a reason for why I never wanted contact with Blake over the years. He always managed to stay independent in whatever his opinion is, but never asked, pushed, or offered much information. Now that I really think about it I don't know why I never found that strange. I'm sure it was because I was so desperate to not know anything about Blake at all that I didn't think anything about it. Just thankful my wishes were respected. But time changes things.

"What do you know?" I boldly ask him.

"Aside from the night you went on and on about loving him and a pregnant Hailey?"

I cringe even after all this time. "Yes."

"Besides the fact that after your graduation things changed? That Blake asked me for your new phone number and email address so many times that we actually came to blows over it one night when we'd both had too much to drink?"

"What? You did?" My eyes widen at the new information.

"You specifically asked that it not be shared with anyone, even Blake. I couldn't and wouldn't go against your wishes. I knew there was a reason, deeper than your mumbled drunken confession."

"Yet you never asked for details or the reason for my actions?"

"I'm not stupid, Sienna. I knew the reason."

"Explain," I demand after looking around to make sure we're still alone. He takes my arm and pulls me to a couple chairs in a corner so we can speak privately. Our dad is involved in various conversations around the room and somehow Jack manages to keep secure the privacy we need in a room full of people. My brother really has grown up.

"I have eyes, you know. I knew you had feelings for Blake over the years. There were times it was obvious and times it wasn't, but I knew the feelings always remained."

"You never said anything."

"No. Not to you."

"What does that mean?"

"It means that I made my feelings about Blake ever pursuing anything with you abundantly clear."

"Wh-wh-what?" I stutter in shock and surprise. I can feel my mouth hanging open but am unable to do anything but stare at him dumbfounded.

"He was my best friend, Sienna. You are my sister. The thought of, well, I wasn't a fan. I told him you were off limits and out of respect and concern for our friendship, he conformed to my wishes. Even though I know it was hard for him at times."

"Hard for him? What do you mean?"

"He had feelings for you too."

"What?" I practically screech and people's heads swing in our direction out of curiosity.

"Shh," he says and I give him a dirty look.

"He did not."

"Yes he did. There were times I thought for sure he was going to ignore everything we ever talked about and do what he wanted. I told him that we wouldn't be friends anymore, that I would tell mom and dad that he wasn't welcome at our house any longer and that I was unequivocally not okay with anything between you."

"I don't understand why you would do that. You had no right."

He shrugs, "I know. I'm sorry. I was protective of you. I was worried about him, About you. About me – maybe mostly me. I couldn't imaging losing my best friend over my sister. And I wasn't mature enough to deal with the idea of my best friend and sister together."

"He was my best friend too. You both were."

"I know. But he was dealing with a lot because of the situation with his family - his dad leaving, his mom drinking - I didn't want you caught up in the mess those things created within him."

"That wasn't your choice."

"I knew he would listen because you, me, our family... we were the refuge he needed when things were hard in his own home. He didn't want to mess that up with you, with our parents."

"Jack..."

He ignores me. It's like now that he's uncorked the bottle he can't stop the flow, "When I knew we had made the decision to join the Army it only affirmed my feelings further. Clearly, I knew the kind of commitment we were making and in turn what it would take from anyone that would choose to be in a relationship with us through that. You'd have to live your life on hold while you got moments in time to spend with someone you love – and then not at your request, but when they're given permission. Availability would be infrequent and that's no life for anyone. Certainly not for my sister."

"Again, that's not a choice you had the right to make for people, Jack. Not for me, Not for Blake. I would have gladly done that. But instead I thought he didn't feel the same way. My heart was broken over and over and over again."

"I'm sorry for the pain you've been through. I had a hand in that. I've wanted to tell you many times. To confess my role. To apologize. But I wanted to do so in person. That's one of the reasons I kept asking you to visit. And then I'd repeatedly justify it...I justified it so long by telling myself my heart was in the right place for both of you, but I know I was merely being selfish."

"I wish you had confessed. In fact, you should have. Also, why do I get the feeling that with the passionate way you talk about the sacrifice someone would have to make... that you had someone that would have been willing to do that for you too?"

He grins and the sight is heartbreaking because of the revealing look on his face, "You've always been a smart one."

"Oh, Jack."

"Look, I'm fine, I'll always be fine, but I can see in your eyes when you look at him that you're still hurting."

"It doesn't matter anymore."

"Doesn't it?"

"No, but thank you for telling me the truth. A lot of things from the past make sense now." He nods and places his arm around me squeezing. And despite the fact that I may regret it, I plunge forward. "Whatever happened with

Hailey and Blake?" I ask bravely even though the thought of the two of them makes my chest squeeze.

"It's not my story to tell, Sienna."

"Did they... did they have a girl or a boy?"

He hesitates and looks at me and flinches when he sees the look on my face. I'm unguarded, my feelings about that situation plain on my face and in my eyes. "A girl," he says but there's more to the story and I can see that on his face.

Not yet done, I ask one more question on my mind, "Why does Blake walk with a limp?"

He cringes and shakes his head, "Again, not my story to tell."

"Well, it seems that Blake and I have some catching up to do."

"That you do," Jack says and we both stand. "I love you, Sienna. Everything I did, it's because of that. But I realize I could have loved you better."

"Please, never make decisions for me again." I try to say it lightly, though the ramifications of his behavior still are overwhelming and crowd my mind. "I don't think either of us could take the fallout. And I have no doubt you'd never like that favor returned."

"Promise. And again, I am truly sorry."

Turning toward the back door that opens to the back-yard where Blake escaped earlier, I make my way knowing I never saw him come inside. It seems it's past time for my past and present to collide whether I like it or not.

Opening the door, I step outside and pause when I see him standing facing some wild flowers in desperate need of taming. His back stiffens when he realizes his private moment has been violated.

I'm about to announce my presence when he says, "What are you doing out here, Sienna?"

The shock of him knowing it's me and him using my full name, stops me in place. "How did you know it was me?"

He laughs without humor and finally turns to face me. A breeze blows stirring the hair at his forehead as his eyes meet mine. "Do you really think you could ever be anywhere near me and I wouldn't know it?"

Taken back by that statement, and unsure how to respond, I ignore it, "How are you doing?"

He laughs again, "What a loaded question."

"I know. I'm sorry. I'm - I'm worried about you."

He looks away from me and I'd give anything to go to him and put my arms around him, but I can't.

"Seven years," he begins, "is a long time. I wasn't sure if I'd see you at all."

"Why wouldn't you? Of course I'd be here. We were... are... friends."

"Is that what we are?" He asks and again I find myself tongue-tied. "Where is he?" he asks and my brow furrows.

"He? Who?"

"The boyfriend," he says.

"Jesse?" my voice cracks in surprise at the question.

"I don't know what the fuck his name is," he says angrily. "Why isn't he with you?"

"How do you even-" I stop because of course the answer is Jack or some gossip monger who wanted to be sure he knew, but his tone and the fact he would even care to know about me is surprising. "There isn't a boyfriend." He looks at me in confusion. "Not anymore."

"What happened?"

"It's a long and rather uninteresting story," I offer.

He nods then begins to walk toward me and I realize he's going to walk past me and back into the house. His limp again makes me curious as to what happened. When he passes me, I blurt out the first thing I think in an effort to stop him, wanting more time with him.

"Jack told me."

He stops. Turns. Looks at me and waits.

I swallow once. Twice. The look in his eyes unreadable.

"Told you *what* exactly?"

"He told me...just told me...that he told you not to pursue a relationship with me. That you had feelings for me. You know... before."

His eyes hold mine and I know a million thoughts run through his mind. I can see them even though I can't define them.

"It doesn't change anything" he shakes his head.

"What? It changes *everything*."

"No. It doesn't. I wasn't good enough for you then anyway, and I'm certainly not good enough for you now. So no, it doesn't change anything."

"Blake-"

"Just drop it, Si."

"I can't," I tell him and the emotion behind those two words can't be contained.

He sighs and relents, "Treehouse, tomorrow? Meet me at six o'clock? I have some things I have to take care of most of the day. Does that work for you?"

"Yes. I'll be there."

He walks away and for the first time in a long time that mustard seed of hope has sprung back to life inside me.

13

I'm early. I got out of work as fast as I could, drove to the house, and without a word to dad or Jack made my way to the treehouse. I haven't been up here for years - I couldn't bring myself to come up - it felt too painful to do so alone.

There's dust in all the corners and the hatch creaked so loud when I pushed it up I'm sure people a town over heard it open. But otherwise, not much has changed. For a short minute I revel at how sound and secure dad must have built it and that he must have preserved the wood to withstand all of the elements this many years. It must have meant as much to him to have provided this for us, as it did for us to have access to it.

I've been a nervous wreck all day. Work kept me busy which meant I was distracted and unable to obsess about it all day, but thoughts still tried to creep in anyway. I couldn't even let myself enjoy the fact we had a great day of production; I was sweating about meeting Blake. About what to say and how to say it. And if I would know if I even should. At some level I am wanting to clear my head and heart. To say all the things I've never gotten a chance to say. Would I really be brave enough to say them now?

"Sienna?"

His voice calling for me makes goosebumps break out over my whole body and tears come to my eyes. How I had missed something as simple as him saying my name. I don't think I realized the full extent of how much I missed having him in my life until the emotions knocked me over like a bulldozer after seeing him again yesterday.

"Hey," I respond and look down and see him through the many leaves and branches between us. "I'm here."

"Can you come down?"

My brow lowers in confusion at the fact that he's not coming up. "Sure."

I open the hatch again, grimacing at the sound again, then make my way down carefully. When I'm close to the ground, he reaches up and helps me the rest of the way.

"Thanks," I smile at him brushing my hands together once my feet are on the ground.

"I, um, wasn't thinking when I said to meet here. It was just automatic, I guess. I brought a blanket. I thought we could sit at the base of the tree."

"Okay," I nod and help him spread out the blanket when he pulls it from under his arm. I watch as he sits and then seems to struggle a bit with his leg, which I find confusing and want to ask about, but I'm so nervous and know I need to wait for him.

He stares out toward his property and I look in the same direction. Rows and rows of wheat blow in the slight breeze. "I would dream about this place when I was away," he says his voice so soft I lean toward him to hear him better. "The funny thing is that my dreams would include things like the wheat field, the treehouse, driving up your driveway, and when I dreamt about having dinner as a family it was with your family - not mine. Jack would be there all the time," his eyes met mine before looking away again, "and you. You were always there." He pauses, swallows, runs his hand through his hair. "It never made me feel bad before, knowing that when I thought about belonging, about family, that it only makes sense that I would think about the place where it always felt like home to me. But now, with mom..."

"Blake," I whisper wishing to offer comfort but not knowing how.

"You shut me out, left me," he says suddenly and it takes me off guard. "I used to *live* for your emails - your letters when you'd write them. They seemed to come at times when I needed them the most. When I had moments of regret for joining the Army at all. When I missed home. When I wasn't sure I could do the next task, conquer the next challenge. When I would have given anything to come back. When I was in a god-forsaken country that became the thing nightmares are made of and saw things I'll never be able to unsee - I would have given anything to have received a single email from you."

"I'm sorry," I choke, his words shocking me with their honesty. "I just-"

"I know. I know you were angry, you were hurt, you were protecting yourself, and I have tried to understand over the years, but hell, Si, I'm fucking pissed off too and I'm not going to pretend not to be."

"I loved you," I choke out and almost immediately I wish I could grab the words from the air and shove them back into my mouth. Especially when his gaze collides with mine. But I push through, "I didn't just love you. I was *in love* with you. And my heart broke over and over."

"I didn't-"

"Mean to? I know. But when I saw Hailey," my throat closes up and I feel the words get trapped. I can still picture that night and I need to clear my throat a couple times to continue. "When I saw her," I say again, "it broke me. In that instant I knew that in order for me to really move on, to let go, to stop holding on to my unreasonable dreams hoping for something that was never going to happen, I needed to cut and run."

"And how did that work out for you?"

I laugh bitterly, "I never really did escape you."

He looks deeply into my eyes and pushes the hair blowing in my face behind my ear. The touch of his fingertips against my skin, makes me tingle. I feel his touch there after he pulls his hand away.

"What, um, what happened with Hailey? I had heard you aren't together," he looks at me curiously, "I overheard my parents talking about it once, but I don't know what happened. Jack said that you have a daughter."

He laughs and it takes me off guard, "There's a lot you don't know, Si."

"Then tell me."

"Why? Why should I?" he asks, and it isn't unkind. I understand why he's asking.

"I understand if you don't want to, but all I can say is that I'm sorry. I was sad, broken, confused and determined to move on. I didn't allow myself to think about how it would make you feel because I was confident it wouldn't matter. You had her."

"Wouldn't matter?" he scoffs at me and the pain in his expression was evident. "It was everything. Don't you get it? I loved you too. I was *in love* with you too."

"No you weren't," I shake my head, tears springing to my eyes.

"Don't tell me how I felt. I know. I know the strength it took to stay away. To always keep you at arms length because you were untouchable. It could never happen, so I'd do whatever it took to honor your brother's request and stay away from you."

Tears roll down my face unchecked. It seems trite but I can't stop them.

"There were moments that were so much harder than others, but then Jack's words would come back and I knew that losing you all would be far worse than having you upset with me for a little while. I couldn't chance losing the love and acceptance of your family. Even if you were upset, or hurt because you thought your feelings weren't returned, at least you were still in my life. The thought of losing you completely was incapacitating, so I made do." He shakes his head and looks at me, "Ironic isn't it?"

"Ironic?"

"I lost you anyway."

"I don't know what to say."

"I don't expect you to say anything. I hate it, but I understand it. I'm angry a bit at you, at myself, at Jack, at life, but again, I know why you made your choice. But while you may not know about me and my life over the last seven years, I know everything about yours."

"Excuse me?"

He laughs and the sound makes my heart flutter. It's been so long since I've heard the sound and I forgot how it makes me feel. "Do you really think I'd let Jack get away with not keeping me informed? He knew better after seeing how I responded to you cutting me off than to ever deny me that. It was all I had left."

"All this time...just lost. Jack had no right."

"No, he didn't. I don't know what's worse to be honest. His request, or my abiding by it."

I'm stunned. So many revelations and my heart feels sad one moment and full of hope the next. What I'm hearing, what he's said is that he's missed me, had feelings for me, was affected by me enough to still be angry at me. Maybe there's still a chance.

"One of the times I came home, I stupidly got drunk and hooked up with Hailey. One night, it was after I had sent you an email after one too many drinks letting myself be honest with you. God, I missed you so much, and I just couldn't lie about how I felt anymore. I told you I wondered what would have happened if Jack hadn't interrupted us the night of our graduation party."

"I remember," I confess and my voice sounds raspy. I remember more than just the email. I remember that night and the feelings come flooding back.

"Well one night I checked my email, wondering if I'd have a response from you. Half excited, half scared out of my mind knowing I said more than I should have. And there it was. Do you remember what you said?"

With everything that I am.

I remember everything between us.

"It said, I think about it too."

"It said more than that. It said 'yours' before you put your name."

"Yes, I remember."

"That one word, it meant everything."

"Then what happened? Your response-"

"I went to respond to you. I was going to lay it all on the line - Jack and his wishes be damned. But then my email sounded and I don't know why but I looked at my inbox.

The subject line of the email captured my attention first. It said, 'Congratulations, Daddy'." My gut churns at those words and I feel sick. "I saw it was from Hailey and I can't explain to you how I felt at that moment. I opened the email and inside was an ultrasound photo she attached."

I nodded, "It just wasn't our time, I guess."

His stare is focused on the wheat field before us but I'm sure he's not really seeing it. He's clearly reliving that night. How it made him feel. I can only imagine the shock.

"I spiraled. I experienced so many emotions I can't even recall them all. Shock. Disbelief. Anger. Shame. Fear. Worry."

"I'm sure it was hard knowing she was in that state and you were so far away."

"I'm not talking about her, Sienna, not entirely. Yes, those are emotions I felt when she told me she was pregnant, but mostly it's how I felt in regards to telling you. To you finding out. Shock was the situation, yes. But I felt disbelief that I had just said all of that to you, that you had just called yourself mine, and I knew it would all disappear because of one evening. I felt shame that I allowed myself to be in the position to begin with. Fear that I'd lose you all together and worry over how you'd react when you found out. My whole world, it didn't revolve around Hailey and the position she found herself in because of our actions, but it circled around what it would do to you. To the us that never even got to begin."

"That's why you didn't respond for a week and when you did…"

"When I did I told you that I never should have sent it. By that time guilt set in. Guilt that my first thoughts were of you and us and not about the baby. I had to be responsible - do the right thing for that child."

"The baby..."

"I was due for some time off and I took it, knowing I had shit to straighten out and it happened to coincide with your graduation which I wanted to attend more than anything. I needed to see you. Even if it was from afar. I never meant for you to find out that way - I initially told Jack I didn't want you to know I was there, but he insisted that he tell you that he sent me in his place. Well, you know how the rest of all that went."

"I do," I say quietly. He turns to look at me, sees the pain in my eyes and immediately takes my hand in his and squeezes it. "What happened next? You said you know about my life but I don't know about yours. What happened with you and Hailey? Do you see your daughter?"

"Hailey lied," he says quietly and at first I'm not sure I heard correctly.

"Lied?" I repeat confused.

"I moved her out to the base where I was stationed in California. She stayed with me and it was tough for a while. Military life isn't easy and it was no secret that I was only with her because of the baby. We didn't get along, she had a difficult time making friends and it certainly wasn't the glamorous life she was expecting - I don't know *what* she was expecting really. All I did was try to make the best of it. I took the best care of her I could."

"I'm sure you did," I tell him feeling as if I should reassure him that I wouldn't expect he'd ever do anything less.

"She knew though. Knew I missed you with everything I had," he turns to me. The look in his eyes freezes me. This time I squeeze his hand and he smiles a little.

"I missed you too. If that counts for anything."

He nods, but doesn't respond to that. Instead he reaches behind him and pulls out his wallet from his back pocket. I look on curiously and then grin when he pulls out a photo of the two of us.

"Oh my gosh, where did you get that?"

It's a picture from the night of prom. One my mom took of Jack, Blake and me. I'm laughing at something and looking up at Blake and he's looking at me too. Jack has been folded to the side - the focus on Blake and me.

"Your mom sent it to me."

"My mom?" I ask softly, tears stinging the back of my throat as my eyes swing from his to the photo.

"It came in a care package she sent once."

"That night was one of the best of my life," I confess.

"One night, Hailey found me looking at this. Well, at a copy of this - I had to request another because she destroyed the first. She was angry, accused me of wanting to be with you and not her and of course she was right, but I couldn't tell her that. I calmed her down and we made the best of things, but then I received orders to Afghanistan. Hailey was only five months pregnant at the time and she didn't take the news of my leaving well. But obviously I had no choice."

"Afghanistan, that's what you meant when you said you've seen things you can't unsee."

He nods, "I can't even really explain the mess it is over there. They sent us to help keep the peace, and we did the best we could."

"I've read about it. I've tried to keep a pulse on all of our dealings with other countries since you and Jack joined. I read about the critical level of kidnappings, hostage taking, landmines and terrorist and insurgent attacks there."

Now I know for a fact that he may be here with me, but part of him is definitely elsewhere. "It's not even describable. I was only there for six months, but it was the longest six months of my life."

"Six months? So you missed the birth of your daughter?"

"I was supposed to be there longer, but things didn't go according to plan." I look at him curiously, waiting for him to explain. "We were sent into a town to check things out. There had been murmurings of covert meetings of terrorists and they wanted us to try to push out any cells. I remember getting ready to knock on the door of a house and a little child - a girl - ran up to some guys in my unit asking for help. She was saying something I couldn't understand, talking so fast and pointing behind her. I don't know what tipped me off, how I suddenly knew what I was seeing, but it didn't matter. I was too late."

"What do you mean?"

His eyes look deeply into mine and the sight takes my breath away - they're haunted by the memories he's reliving. I almost want to tell him to stop because it's clear they're bringing him pain. I reach out and touch the part of his leg that's closest to me, and freeze.

He freezes too. Emotions, too many to count, cross over his features. "The child," he continues softly, "was a decoy. She was wearing a bomb strapped to her chest. I called out," his voice sounds raspy now, like the words he's saying are scraping out of his throat against their will. "But it was too late. I just remember a flash of white. Searing pain."

His limp.

The hardness that's not natural I'm feeling now.

The look in his eyes.

I know.

I know what happened. "Oh, Blake," I whisper, sadness and pain wrenching my heart at the thought of what he's been through.

Without a word he reaches down and lifts his pant leg. A prosthesis appears all the way up to just under his knee. "I didn't handle losing it well. I was angry - thoroughly pissed off and mourning my friends. I was stuck in a hospital bed for a while, Hailey would come and visit but I could see her getting angrier and angrier each time. I'll never forget the look on her face when she first saw..."

I hate her. I hated her before but I hate her with a fiery passion now. She better hope I never see her.

"I required a lot of care at first. The initial prosthetic didn't work. Too painful, uncomfortable. Missing a limb requires relearning how to walk, to move, in a way you wouldn't expect. There's a new balance, rhythm, pace to get used to. It's hindering in ways you don't want it to be and denial is a real and heavy thing. I didn't know you could grieve for a body part. So many things I didn't know."

"I can't even imagine. You're so strong, Blake. You amaze me."

He laughs sardonically, "Right. Strong. No. I was a mess. I'll never forget the day that Hailey came home from... I don't know shopping or something. She had... Peyton in her arms and said she needed a diaper change..."

Peyton. His daughter's name is Peyton.

"I wanted to help. I stood, began crossing the room with my crutches when my gait got out of sequence with my crutches and I got caught in midair – then fell. Hard. To the ground."

My heart goes out to him at the thought.

"I was embarrassed, struggled to get up and Hailey... well she was angry. She exploded. Told me that she was sorry but that this wasn't working. That she had a confession to make, that Peyton, wasn't mine," he choked out.

"What?"

"She told me that she couldn't be my caretaker and her

daughter's too. That she needed to make the right choice for her and it wasn't me."

"She was lying, right?"

"I thought so, accused her of it, but she had gotten a paternity test done with a sample of my blood - god knows there was enough of it around during my recovery and she showed it to me. I am not her father. Having to choose between me and her actual father, apparently I was the better choice at the time, until this," he says gesturing to his leg.

"I don't even know what to say. An apology just seems inadequate."

"It was a long time ago. It is what it is."

"And now? What have you been doing since then?"

"I'm retired from the military obviously, but I still help teach new recruits. I like it, it keeps me busy. It's not something I have to do, but I want to."

"So what now, Blake?"

"What do you mean?" his brow furrows in confusion.

"Are you...are you with someone now - romantically?"

"No," he says hesitantly.

"Blake?"

"Yeah?"

"I think we've waited long enough, don't you?"

He shakes his head in confusion, "What do you mean?"

I put my mouth on his. The kiss is soft at first, just a meeting of our lips, like they are getting acquainted first, then I add more pressure. He makes a sound in the back of his throat, part surprise, part need and his lips part. I take advantage and deepen the kiss and he matches my intensity move for move.

Without breaking contact, I straddle his lap. I can't believe I'm being so bold, but what do I have to lose? He's not with anyone and he confessed he loved me once - maybe he still does. Maybe he never stopped, like I never stopped loving him. Is there hope for us?

Pulling away from him gently, I look into his eyes and place my hands on his cheeks. His eyes squeeze close. When he opens them and looks at me, I smile. His hands grip my sides and he doesn't push me away.

"Do you still wonder?"

"Wonder?"

"What would have happened if we weren't interrupted?"

His eyes widen and before he can say anything, I put my lips on his again. I pour everything I'm feeling into that kiss. How I've missed him all this time. How my heart aches for what he's been through. How I'd give anything for one big do-over.

His hands leave my sides and travel up my back and then dive into my hair. His kiss is fire. Passion pours into me and I know, *I know,* that there will never be anyone else for me. No one has ever made me feel this way. I push the softest part of me into the hardest part of him and his groan excites me.

My hands travel down his chest and to his stomach and then suddenly, I'm no longer sitting on him anymore, I'm seated next to him once more.

"Wh-" I look over at Blake and see his chest rising and falling sharply.

"That shouldn't have happened."

"What? Why? You said you're not with anyone. Neither am I."

"Sienna, we can't do this. We can't be together," he says quietly and with pain reflected in his eyes.

"What? Why? I don't understand. Is it because I live here and you live in California? I mean, yeah that will make things hard, but long distance has worked for people before."

"No."

"No?"

"Sienna, I'm not... you deserve better than someone like me."

"Someone like you?" I shake my head in confusion. "I don't have any idea what you mean."

With a little bit of difficulty he stands and limps as he takes a few steps away from me. His head is down, hands on his hips and he appears to be trying to compose himself.

"Hailey was a lot of things, but she was right about one thing."

"Oh, please. Do tell. This should be interesting," I say with sarcasm while feeling ire begin to rise inside of me like a tsunami gathering strength before it crashes to shore.

"I'm not... I'm not a complete man."

"What?" I ask disbelief freezing me as I stare at him sure that I misheard what he said.

"When she left, she said that I'm only half a man now. One that will always need taken care of on some level. I'm not good enough for you, Si. This can't happen. I won't let it - no matter....no matter..."

"No matter what?"

He ignores the question, "I can only be your friend, again, if you'll have me."

I shake my head as if it will dislodge the words that have penetrated my ears, "I'd say you're joking, but this isn't fucking funny."

"I wasn't trying to be."

"You losing part of your leg does not make you less of a man. That's ludicrous."

"I disagree."

"You're wrong."

"No, I'm not, and I won't entertain a discussion about this further."

"Excuse me?"

"Look, I've had a lot of time to get used to, the way things are now. You just found out. You think you can deal with this, but you can't."

"Don't tell me what I can and can't deal with. You're not the only one that's been through some hard things over the years."

"I know. I wasn't trying to disregard your feelings and your losses. And I've never gotten to tell you in person that I'm sorry about the loss of your mom."

"Thank you, but that has nothing to do with anything right now."

"No, but it needed to be said nevertheless."

"Blake, we need to talk about this."

"I can't. Not right now. I need to get back to the house. Mandy and I are having a late dinner."

"Blake," I take a step toward him and reach out. He jerks away from my touch, making me freeze into place, hurt lancing my heart.

"I'll talk to you later, okay?" he says and I can do nothing but watch him as he walks away from me while pain of a different kind enters my heart. Pain that he would think for one second that he's not good enough for anyone, let alone me, takes my breath away.

Well, he's about to get up close and personal with the woman I've become since he's seen me last. I smile to myself, because he's never going to know what hit him by the time I'm done. It's way past time for things to finally work out for us. I refuse to lose him again. I barely survived it the first time.

14

$\mathcal{I}$t's been two days since Blake walked away from me. I've gone to his house and pounded on the door demanding he talk to me, but he won't answer. Maybe he wants me to believe he's not there, but given his rental car is in the driveway, it's a dead giveaway. I even got Jack to call him and then took the phone from him when he answered, but I just got a brusque, "Not right now, Sienna," which was very frustrating.

It's been a long day at work. I've participated in a couple meetings meant to motivate by brainstorming and collaborating with fellow practice managers. Normally they're a great way to kick start a week and leave me feeling pumped up and motivated, but I'm struggling to hang onto any kind of positive feeling right now. Blake's attitude and shutting me out is really messing with my head, not to mention my heart.

Focusing is difficult but I throw myself into my day and help train a new assistant, respond to emails, interact with patients, decide on a marketing strategy for the month, and work on organizing the upcoming team meeting among other things.

I'm grateful when the day finally comes to a close and decide before I go home to head by Blake's once more but drive on by when I don't see his rental car there. Not feeling like going home, I decide to make a stop on my way and swing into Vanessa's driveway.

She and her little family don't live too far away from me. When I knock on the door I'm not waiting long before my friend stands before me with no makeup, a shirt that has a substance on it that I don't recognize with a tired look in her eyes, but a big grin on her face at the sight of me.

"Sienna! Hi!"

"Hi. Sorry I didn't call first."

She grabs my arm and pulls me inside, "You never have to call first. My door is open to you always, you know that."

"Yeah well, it's dinner time. I don't want to interfere."

"You're not. Scott's got Sam in the bath and I have a few peaceful moments to myself."

"You sure I didn't interrupt you going to take your own bath or shower?" I grimace at her in mock horror and she smacks my arm.

"One day when you're in this position I plan on plastering my face to the glass windows of your home so I can enjoy the pure entertainment of you slowly going insane. Meanwhile, I'll just laugh and tell you it's not so funny now, is it?"

"Well, that's fair," I shrug and we laugh.

"So, spill it."

"What do you mean? Why would you think I have anything to spill?"

"Oh please. I made one trip to the grocery store for milk

and got an ear full all about Blake being here - which I totally called by the way…"

"Yes you did and thank you again for the heads up."

"You're welcome. I heard all about how great he looks, how bad Virginia looked… well dead…"

"Vanessa!"

"What? I'm just repeating what they said."

I sigh and grab the chip bag from her counter, "Go on," I tell her and place a BBQ chip in my mouth and chew happily.

"Hungry?" Vanessa teases me when I hum in happiness.

"I was so busy… well keeping busy… that I didn't each much today."

"Well, help yourself," she says and snags a few of her own out the bag to munch. "I heard how handsome your brother looked."

"True. It's the uniform - the ladies love it. According to him anyway."

"Anyway, I guess Blake has been all over town getting his mom's affairs in order and I know that my best friend has to be feeling all kinds of things, so why don't you fill me in on everything I've missed."

So I do. I tell her everything from how it felt walking into the funeral and seeing Blake again after so long. How angry he was when we briefly spoke. The things Jack told me and how it lead to the conversation I had with Blake by the tree-house a couple days ago. Through it all she's a rapt audience. Scott popped his head out once and saw our intense conversation, smiled, waved, and disappeared with Sam again. I'll owe him one - busting in on their evening like this.

"So, what are you going to do?" she asks with eyes wide.

"Well, isn't that the million dollar question?"

"It's sad, that he would think that way," she muses.

"It's heartbreaking. I just don't know how to get through to him."

We're quiet for a moment and then Vanessa's eyes get big. "I know that look. What are you thinking?"

"What did he tell you he lived for when he was away? The way he still felt connected to home when he wasn't here."

"You mean when I'd email him?"

She nods, "When you'd email him."

It isn't long before I'm sharing the same wide-eyed look. I jump up, and she does too, I throw my arms around her and squeeze. "You're brilliant. I love you. I'll call you later."

"You better! And I want all the credit after the sweet, sweet, love, got it?"

"Deal!" I smile and laugh. "Give Scott and Sam a hug for me."

"You got it."

I drive straight home, my mind already swirling with all the things I want and need to say. Could she be right? Could emailing him be the way to reach him? To get him to pay attention and actually hear what I have to say? And where do I even start?

Not knowing any other way, I start at the beginning, I start where we left off.

Dear Blake,

Leaving you that night, getting in Vanessa's car and driving away was one of the hardest things I've ever done. When the emotions I was holding in threatened to break me I did everything I could to push them away. I went to the graduation party, like I planned. I pretended to have a good time, even though I was broken and lost on the inside. I kept telling myself I was doing the right thing, that the only way to move on and to let go was to cut all ties. I lost count of all the times I thought about texting you or emailing you. All the times I almost broke and got in touch with you anyway, but stubbornness is a funny thing. It's definitely one of the things I got from my mom that I both love and hate about myself. I'd like to tell you that if I had to do it all over again I would have made a different decision, but the truth is that I probably would do the same thing again. Looking back I realize that it made me stronger, made me realize that I can get through loss, that everything about who I am isn't tied up in my feelings about a person even though sometimes it seemed like I didn't know where I ended and you began. But know, that not one day went by where I didn't miss you. That the loss of you wasn't felt. Even though it was my own doing.

    Yours,

    Sienna

Dear Blake,

    College was pretty fun, but hard at the same time. As you know, I always planned on leaving our town if I could - knowing there's so much to explore out there and wanting to be a part of it. That didn't work out like I thought it would, but that's okay. I stayed in Montana for college and so did Vanessa. That meant our friendship only became stronger, and together we learned we really had forged a friendship that would last a lifetime. We made other friends too, ones we still stay in touch with even now. All of us would go out together and through them I discovered a love for partying, laughing, and drinking and oh my gosh sometimes there was way too much drinking. For instance, did you know that after five shots I had better stop drinking or I suddenly think it's a good idea to take off my clothes? It's true. I'd feel like my body was on fire and needed air on my skin. How do I know this? Because those so-called friends have photo evidence. Maybe I'll show you one day.

Yours,

Sienna

Dear Blake.

One time, I met a boy in one of my classes. He flirted with me and asked me out constantly until I found myself saying yes. We spent every minute together for a while and I fancied myself 'in love.' One day we were supposed to meet for coffee at our favorite place on campus, but he didn't show up. Worried, I went to his place and as I got to the door saw him kissing a girl goodbye as she left his place disheveled and well... let's just say she looked like she'd been rode well. When he saw me, he tried to make all kinds of excuses, but I never spoke to him again. The sting of betrayal hurt and it took me a little while to get over, but it also taught me what true love should look like. Like the way I love you.

Yours,

Sienna

Dear Blake,

Remember how we used to despise our English teacher

Mrs. Dooberry in high school? Not only because saying her last name was almost impossible to do so without smiling and wanting to laugh, but because she made us read the worst books and then made us write five hundred word essays. You know it's funny - those stupid expectations she had about how a paper should be written made a couple college classes a piece of cake. Guess she knew what she was doing after all.

Yours,

Sienna

Dear Blake,

I hate you. Why did you choose her? Why wasn't I enough for you? I miss you more than I can even express. Some days I am so great at pushing thoughts of you away, I can go without thinking about you, but that's when you creep into my dreams. Dreams of what our lives could have been like if you had only seen me. Dreams of what your life is probably like now without me. This hurts. So much. Sometimes, I wish I could go back and do that night differently.

Yours,

Sienna

Dear Blake,

If I had sent you an email when my mom passed - I know it would have read like this.

My mom is gone. They say it happened fast, that she felt no pain and it's completely irrational but I feel angry about that. I'm angry because she got to slip from this world pain-lessly while leaving an emptiness in my heart so vast I don't know that I'll ever recover. It feels hard to breathe. Is it because I can't live in a world without her in it? Did she take all the oxygen with her because I'm suffocating. I think irrational things like did she know how much I loved her? Did she know that I thanked God that he gave me to her? That watching the love between her and my dad is what makes me want a genuine relationship so desperately myself? Why didn't I tell her I loved her more? Spend more time with her especially on those days when I took time for myself and pushed her aside, always thinking there would be another time. Do you think she forgives me for my selfishness; for all the times I was inconsiderate and ungrateful? Do you think she was proud of me? That she also thanks God that he gave me to her? How do we do this without her? How will I ever stop feeling so lost, so empty? My dad sits and stares and I wonder what's going through his mind? Is he reliving their life? Or is he imagining all the things they didn't get to do together? Does he have regrets too? I wish you were here. I wish I could ask you these things or that you would just hold me in your arms and make me feel at least for a little while that everything will be okay. Because right now, I can't imagine it ever will be again.

Yours,

Sienna

Dear Blake,

I'm angry. I had plans. I had things I wanted to do. A world I wanted to discover and explore. Remember that list of places I told you about? I still want to see them - desperately. I hate this town sometimes. The gossips, the way everyone knows everything about everyone. I'm mad at you. I'm mad at Jack. Why did you both have to decide to leave me? Couldn't one of you have at least stayed? Made a different choice? Because who else is left now to pick up the pieces? Dad needs help. He can't do this. He's lost. He's floundering. He misses her and it's breaking him. He can't - or won't - keep up on things like he should. I'm leaving college, dropping out, because he's more important. I need to help him, keep him from losing everything. He's behind on... everything. I need to be there for him, run things, get everything back on track and I can't do that and go to school full-time too. I feel selfish because I'm angry. Then, the next minute I know this is my choice and not one he necessarily wants me to make. But he doesn't tell me not to do this. Periodically, I want to pretend it isn't happening, that it's all been a bad dream, and keep living my life the way I want to. I want to follow my dreams - once I determine what exactly they are - and not have to worry about anything or anyone else. I'm young. Why should it be my job to take care of my parent? And I'm still healing too. I miss her too. How am I going to do this? Can I even do this? I have to. He needs me. That's all that matters.

Yours,

Sienna

Dear Blake,

Do you still think about me? I shouldn't, but I still think about you. I try not to but I compare any man I date to you. Isn't it stupid? You and I.. we never had anything. We never even kissed. My feelings for you were immature... weren't they? Am I just using the memory of you to make excuses when things don't work out? When I'm unable to connect with a man the way I wish I could? Maybe something's wrong with me... am I broken? Am I incapable of having a relationship, of feeling deeply? Why do I let an old unre-quited crush dictate my life now? Why have I built this up to being bigger than it ever was?

I don't know who I belong to.

Sienna

Dear Blake,

He cares about me. We have a good time together. We laugh, talk about places we'd like to go, things we'd like to do, accomplishments we hope to realize. He's a good man. I could see myself being happy with him, having a future, maybe a child or two, a house and dog. But something's missing. When he touches me, kisses me, holds me, I don't feel passion. I don't feel whole. How long will I continue to let the ghost of what never was between you and me haunt my life now? Will I ever let myself be happy?

Yours even though I shouldn't be,

Sienna

And on it goes. I send him emails about everything he missed. Feelings big, small, insignificant or ones that are absolutely everything - they contain my whole heart and all the truths - even if they don't put me in the best light - espe-cially those. Those are important. I don't hold anything back. I tell him all the things I wish I had been able to tell him had he still been here - had things been different. I send them one at a time - all the emails he may have received from me had we kept in contact. And then, I send him the email of all emails. I lay it all on the line.

. . .

Dear Blake,

Did you know that after I met you the day that I fell from the tree house everything in my life suddenly became defined by one thing? Everything became before I met you, and after I met you. It's funny though because now I can hardly remember any of the before because the afters consume me – it's like nothing existed until you walked into my life. That day I had no idea that you had started the process of ingraining yourself into my heart, but you did. Little by little, day by day, another chapter created another story and that story added to the book of us.

All of the emails I shared contain pieces of me. Good pieces, bad pieces, embarrassing pieces, broken pieces. Do they make me less of a woman? Less worthy of love, happiness, completeness? Do they make me less attractive? Less desirable?

You told me that you losing your leg makes you less of a man, because it's a broken piece of you, because maybe as a result of it you aren't the same, - not as 'whole'. Maybe things aren't as easy as they used to be or exactly what you thought they would be. I think that the same thing could be said for all of us I'm sure, certainly I feel like that too given experiences I've endured. Experiences like losing my mom, feeling trapped into helping my dad and momentarily forgetting that doing so was ultimately my choice. Giving up my college experience and education, continuing to live in this town and losing parts of myself. These selfish, embarrassing, angry, frustrating moments are all broken pieces of me too. By your standards that makes me...what? Incomplete? Lacking? Deficient? Less than worthy to be enmeshed in the life of someone I love?

I certainly hope not.

You don't understand how I see you or the depth of my

feelings for you. You are more than enough. The total package. My feelings aren't conditional, predicated on your physical stature or characteristics. I am not so vain, so superficial. I love you because of your heart, because of the man you are. I love the freckle under your left eye, the way you laugh with your whole body when you find something really funny. I love how you've always been caring and protective of me. I love how you cared for Mandy when your Mom couldn't. I love the fact that my family is your family. I love your loyalty. I love how you've always treated me with respect and value. I love the way you run your hands through your hair when you're nervous or stressed. I love how you've honored our country, that you gave up the likely role of a popular college jock – and then, literally a piece of yourself to serve it. But, Blake, I don't have blinders on either. I know you also have flaws and imperfections. Need me to name a few? Fine. How about how you can overthink things? You can be ridiculously overprotective, argue a point to death, are just as scared of spiders as I am, have a weird fascination with eating ketchup on all your meats and do you even floss? But the thing is, all of your experiences, characteristics, attitudes and attributes make you the man you are today - the man I've always loved. No matter what.

Regardless of never having taken vows, you can consider me all in, for better or worse. I made that decision a long time ago. No matter what you say, you can't change my mind. I won't let you. So, how dare you suggest that I'm not capable of loving you as you are. That some physical change would alter my impression of you, my thoughts toward you. Because it can't. I have always seen you with my eyes wide open, in each stage of life, and accepted and wanted you as you were – and now is no exception. I take you as you are because loving you is a privilege. These things that we've been through, all of the tragedies, they're all perfect, because they led us back to each other and if you can't see that, I feel sorry for you. I hope one day you do, and until then, you know where to find me.

ALWAYS Yours,

Sienna

I laid it all out there. Said everything I wanted to say. The ball is in his court and while the thought of him remaining steadfast and stubborn to his way of thinking pains me, I know that I fully expressed myself and feel some level of comfort having done so.

When I look at the clock, I realize it's very late. I grab a snack and force it down having missed dinner and knowing I haven't had much of an appetite lately. I go through my nightly routine and collapse into bed. It's far easier to fall asleep than I expected it would be.

Blake's just out of reach. I keep calling his name over and over, my hand reaching out to him, but he's beyond me. He goes through a door and I yank on the handle, but it's locked, I can't open it. I begin banging on the door, desperate to get through, desperate to reach him. He has to hear me, has to listen to what I have to say.

Suddenly I sit upright in bed, gasping for breath, realizing I was dreaming. Then I also understand that the banging is not just in my mind, it's in my reality too.

I fumble my way out of bed realizing that the bang is coming from my front door; someone is on my porch. Squinting at my clock I see it's three in the morning and my heart stalls in my chest for a minute worried about who it could be and what they might want at this time of the night. I proceed to answer with caution.

Hurrying, I yell, "I'm coming. I'm coming."

I flip on the porch light and look out the peephole and my breath stalls in my chest as I yank the door open and blink several times wondering if I'm still dreaming.

Blake.

15

*M*y heart stalls in my chest.

He's here. Blake is here. He stares and me and his eyes take a journey from the tips of my toes to the top of my head. I realize that I'm only wearing a tiny tank top and short shorts that don't leave a lot to the imagination.

The fire in his eyes makes me realize that perhaps for the first time he's looking at me completely unguarded and holy hell batman, I know without a single doubt that Blake finds me attractive.

"Hi," I say awkwardly.

"Can-" his throat sounds dry and he clears it and tries again, "Can I come inside?"

"Oh, yeah. Sorry. Of course," I say when I realize he's still on the porch and I'm leaning against the door stupidly staring at him.

He walks inside and I close the door. He steps into my house, pauses, and looks around curiously. I realize he's never seen the home I've created for myself, which makes me wonder, "How did you know where I live?"

He laughs softly, "Jack. All I'll say is that he's pretty pissed off right about now and probably trying to fall back asleep as we speak."

I return the slightly uncomfortable laugh imagining my angry brother.

It quiets and we stare at one another.

Life seems to stand at a complete pause.

I feel like we're on the verge of something big - something we can't come back from. I'm aware of every breath – mine and his – and even the slightest moves he makes. I feel like he wants something from me, but I've no clue what it is and I still feel empty - I already gave him all the words I have.

"Did you want to sit?"

He shakes his head, "No, I don't want to sit."

Okay, standing it is then.

"Do you want to go to the kitchen? I can get you something to drink."

He shakes his head again, "I don't want a drink."

We pause longer. I feel a large amount of air release from my own lungs, unaware that I was holding my breath.

"What *do* you want? It's three o'clock in the morning and you're here for some reason, I presume. What is it?"

I cross my arms over my chest as if doing so will protect me from whatever he's going to say. Fear of repeated rejection quickly washes over me and I suddenly feel cold.

He looks at me, holding my gaze. Oh, those unchanging, captivating eyes. They look like the grass and trees before a rain storm. That moment when everything looks so green and peaceful, no sign that in moments a flood may open and drench the earth.

"I have some things I want to say."

I nod and brace myself.

"I missed you too," he says softly. "I want you to know that I felt the loss of you too. Every day. And those photos, the ones of you taking your clothes off when you're drinking, I want to see them."

I laugh – a brief, nervous giggling laughter that catches me off-guard, not expecting those comments or the change in conversation.

"I want to have shots with you, party with you, dance with you."

He takes one step toward me but stops.

"And the guy that hurt you? Betrayed you? I want his name. I have connections you can't possibly imagine," he says so dead serious that I feel a shiver run up my spine at the dangerous tone to his voice.

"Mrs. Dooberry," his lips curl in amusement, "how do you even remember her?"

I smile a little as understanding dawns. He's responding to each of my emails. He read them. He read all of them.

His face grows serious again and he takes a few steps toward me, closer, this time taking my upper arms in his hands. "Your mom knew you loved her. I'm convinced that moms know those things in their souls. It doesn't matter how many times you did or didn't say it, they can feel it, they know it. And proud of you? I think maybe, just maybe she was more proud of you than you could imagine and even more than me. Yes, me. And that's saying a lot because damn I couldn't be prouder of you. Proud of the woman you were, the one you've become, and all the happiness and joy that I know you brought to her life and those in your circle. I'm sorry I wasn't here to hold you and to love you through losing her. I know that you'll feel the loss of her forever, but she'll always be in your heart, in your memories, and I'm here now. I want to accompany you through the rest of that journey. And share my own."

I nod, unable to say a word as unshed tears clog my throat.

"The way you felt about taking care of your dad, it's understandable. It has to be difficult. Yet, how generous of you to trade your needs and dreams to take care of him and help him through the recovery from his loss when your load was already so heavy. He is blessed with a very special daughter. But we all know that. I'm sorry I wasn't here to tell you that then too, so just another thing I want to be sure I say now."

He lets go of my hands and the momentary separation makes me feel sad until his hand cups the side of my face and he waits for my eyes to meet his.

"I need to make something very clear. I didn't choose her," he says staring into my eyes. "No one can compare to you. I settled. I took the easy way out or what I thought was the right solution, the right thing to do but it was anything but right. And I'm sorry. I'd give anything to go back and make a choice, *the* choice, *the right* choice."

I bite my lower lip, trying to hold in the emotion.

"Si" he whispers softly, "I also need you to know that I saw you. Know that. I couldn't stop seeing you. I've *always* seen you. Every day, every conversation, every shared interaction and event. I could describe you in great detail - not merely your beauty and physical attributes, but your spirit, your heart, the person you are. I saw you when I was here and when I wasn't, it was all I could think about – those thoughts kept me sane and stable and whole in spirit. I more than saw you. I wanted you. I needed you. I still do."

His thumb brushes the side of my face, his eyes fall to

my mouth, then meet mine again. "And you were questioning if we ever had anything, had truly meant anything to
each other? Thought maybe you remembered it to be more
than it really was? You didn't, because if that were the case, I
wouldn't have felt it too. That we didn't speak of it, act on it,
did not make it less real. Hell, the fact that you weren't able
to be with the other man that loved you, well thank fuck,
that's just evidence…and good thing it never went anywhere
because then I'd have to call on those connections again."

He smiles when I laugh softly and roll my watery eyes.

"I love you," he says.

Three. Simple. Words.

Three little words that mean everything.

How my heart has wanted to hear those words.

I open my mouth to respond in kind, but he places a
finger over my lips. "There are so many things I love about
you. How you love with your whole heart. Your captivating,
sweet and at times, flirtatious smile. How proud you are of
your family, your love for animals, your loyalty and kindness. The freckle right here," he says brushing the top of my
lip and repeating words I said to him, "and the reminder of
the fall you took here," he says brushing the other side of
mouth and it makes me remember the time he almost
kissed me years ago.

"The way you bite your lip when you're nervous; how
you slightly scrunch up your nose and murmur "mmm"
when you really enjoy something you're eating; how smart
and yet, how practical you are; how extremely beautiful.
Being loved *by you* is a privilege."

"You don't know who you belong to?" He asks referring
to how I ended one of my emails. "I'll tell you. You belong to
me. Now. And always."

"You mean it?" I ask, afraid to hope.

He laughs, "I may not have claimed you before, out loud, but in my heart, that's always been the case. I couldn't wait one more minute to tell you - to show you. There's no doubt that I mean it, that I'm sure."

He smiles softly, looks at my mouth, then puts his mouth on mine. His lips are soft, the kiss firm and exploring. He pulls on my hair gently and my head naturally follows backward, deepening our kiss. With a newfound confidence, I pull away from him and take his hand and lead him without a word to my bedroom.

We undress each other. He stiffens slightly as I remove his jeans, demonstrating what I interpret as a momentary concern about his leg prosthesis. I take the hand that he placed on his jeans to stop me and softly kiss it holding his gaze with my own. I trust that my response and look convey the pride knowing what he endured for his beliefs and moreover, for what he's overcome to still be here. I show him with my words, my lips, my hands and with my body how much I love him. How there is nothing about him that isn't beautiful, whole, or desirable. I tell him and let him show me that he's more than enough man for me as we become one.

After we finish, laying face to face, his fingers trail up and down my back lazily. My eyes are so heavy, but I don't want to fall asleep. I'm afraid to. I don't want to wake up and find out this has all been just a sweet dream.

"I forgot one thing," he whispers.

"Mhm?" I can't form words.

"Remember those places you told me years ago you want to go? I want to take you there. To each of them."

Smiling, I respond with a demand, "Tell me again."

"I love you," he says knowing what I want.

"I'll never tire of hearing it," I smile, eyes finally falling closed, happy, content, confident in our love.

He places a kiss to my lips, "I'll never stop saying it."

EPILOGUE

"How much further?" I ask with a smile in my voice.

"We're almost there," Blake responds, the tone of his voice laced with mischief.

When I got home from work tonight, he waited for me to change and then told me he wanted to take me somewhere. It's a surprise. I was all for it, excited and curious. Then he made me put a blindfold on.

The suspense is killing me.

The last several months have been a whirlwind. I helped Blake and Mandy clean and do minor repairs on their childhood house that has stood empty since Virginia's death to prepare it for being sold. I thought it would be hard for them to part with it, but Blake said that it didn't have many great memories and that he had spent more time at my home than his own and that he was actually quite relieved to finalize the transaction.

Blake also made it clear in no uncertain terms that he would be leaving his home in California and returning to

Mason Creek. I challenged his decision since I knew he loved his job, and was highly confident I could find work at a dental office there. We discussed it several times and my willingness to do so was genuine; frankly, I was willing to be anywhere as long as we were together. But he wouldn't hear of it saying my dad was in Mason Creek, that all of his best memories are here, and then, reminding me – as if that was necessary - that we fell in love here. How could I argue?

His hand is in mine and his thumb continually brushes across the top of my hand. The transitions have been going astoundingly well. Things between us have been a dream. We are more than making up for lost time - we can't get enough of each other. Loving him is a dream, so much so that sometimes I'm still afraid I'm going to wake up and find out all of this didn't happen. I've woken up in a cold sweat a couple times after having nightmares about just that. Each time, Blake has held and soothed me with words of love until I calmed down.

The car stops and I turn my head toward him and he laughs softly.

"What's funny?"

"You look adorable."

"What are we doing? Where are we?" I try to pry information from him.

"Hold on a few minutes."

He opens the car door, leaves my side and the door closes. I hear the trunk open, then close and then I sit in silence waiting.

The air hits my skin as he opens the car door, "Alright love, I'm going to help you turn and get out of the car."

"Okay," I giggle at the absurdity of whatever he's doing.

He helps me walk a few steps and I feel grass tickle my ankles.

"Alright, you can take off the mask and open your eyes now," he instructs.

I obey and smile when as my eyes open. He's brought me to the same spot we came the night of prom. Near the bridge I love and where we ate burgers and spent time together.

"What are we doing here?" I ask and then turn around to find Blake down on one knee. My hands fly to my mouth in surprise and my eyes water immediately.

"Sienna Torres," he begins.

"Yes." I answer impatiently and he laughs out loud throwing his head back and I smile widely.

"What if I was going to ask you to promise to eat burgers with me for the rest of our lives."

"I'd say yes."

"What if I was just going to ask you to get a dog with me?"

"I'd say yes," he laughs his eyes sparkling.

"I love you. Finding our way to each other has been quite the journey but being with you, living my life with you - it all feels like a dream. There are days I wake up and turn to you to reassure myself that you're still there, that I didn't imagine all of it," I smile and nod knowing exactly how he feels. "You are my home. I never feel more complete, more whole, than when I'm with you. I want to spend the rest of my life with you. Consider me all in, for better or worse," he says repeating my written words and it makes me smile wide. "Will you marry me?"

"Yes. A hundred times, yes."

He laughs and puts a gorgeous ring on my finger.

He takes me in his arms and kisses me.

My life felt incomplete for so long, like a lost boat in a raging storm trying to find its way to shore.

Though lost and tossed around, I always knew the direction I was to go and so glad I never gave up.

He's my anchor, my home, my perfect tragedy.

My broken heart, now mended by his love.

ACKNOWLEDGMENTS

Thank you so much to C.A. Harms and all the authors in the Mason Creek series collaboration. This was such an amazing project to be part of and I thank you for including me.

To my mom, thank you as always for being an amazing editor. You're an imperative part of my writing journey and I'm so lucky to do this with you because you help bring out the best in me and my characters. Thanks also for working within the insane timeline I created. I love you.

Georgia, thank you for reading this every step of the way and cheering me on. You helped motivate me and kept me going when I wanted to give up and didn't believe in myself. As always getting to bounce ideas and brainstorm with you is one of my favorite parts of this process. I miss our coffee dates though so much! MOVE BACK!

To my family, I'm so sorry that the house is a nightmare, for all the times we ran out of milk and... well everything. For the fact that I haven't cooked dinner in... ages, and that I've become a shadow of a person these last several weeks while I tried to manage working full-time and meeting this deadline. I love you to the moon! Now go ahead and make a list of all the things I can cook for you!

To my readers, the road back to writing has been a long one. So many obstacles made getting my writing mojo back seem like a finish line I'd never cross again. Thank you for your patience, your words of encouragement and for being as excited as I am about this release. I hope you loved it as much as I adore all of you!

ABOUT THE AUTHOR

Author Jennifer Miller was born and raised in Chicago, Illinois but now calls Arizona home. After winning a school writing contest at the young age of nine, when she wrote a book about a girl and her pet unicorn (her spirit animal), she dreamed of writing a book of her own. The important lesson she learned about dreams is that they don't simply fall into your lap - you have to chase them yourself. Her greatest role however is that of a wife and mother. When she's not writing you'll likely find her loudly cheering on her daughters at their basketball games, spending time with those she loves, or up to shenanigans with her bestie. For more information about Jennifer Miller, please visit www.-jennifermillerwrites.com

NEXT IN THE MASON CREEK SERIES

Perfect Escape by Cary Hart

BUY NOW

Charlee was looking for a place to nurse her broken heart, and Mason Creek was the picture-perfect escape.

Small town life was just a temporary Band-Aid, until sexy single dad Grady gave her a reason to stay... and a second chance at happiness.

THE MASON CREEK COLLECTION

Perfect Risk #1 by C.A. Harms

Perfect Song #2 by Lauren Runow

Perfect Love #3 by A.M. Hargrove

Perfect Night #4 by Terri E. Laine

Perfect Tragedy #5 by Jennifer Miller

Perfect Escape #6 by Cary Hart

Perfect Summer #7 by Bethany Lopez

Perfect Embrace #8 by Kaylee Ryan

Perfect Kiss #9 by Lacey Black

Perfect Mess #10 by Fabiola Francisco

Perfect Excuse #11 by A.D. Justice

Perfect Secret #12 by Molly McLain 12

Full stories, by 12 different authors, all linked together by one small town in Montana. From first loves to old flames, this small town is big on second chances and new beginnings. A picture-perfect postcard town, where everyone feels at home... and everybody under the Montana sky knows your business. Get lost here... find yourself here. Welcome to Mason Creek.

Made in the USA
Coppell, TX
28 April 2025

48786594R00127